MURDER ON MOLOKA'I

A Surfing Detective Mystery

Includes a new essay by the author:
"The Making of Murder on Moloka'i"

Other Surfing Detective books
by Chip Hughes

WIPEOUT!

KULA

MURDER ON MOLOKA'I

A Surfing Detective Mystery

CHIP HUGHES

SLATE RIDGE PRESS

SLATE RIDGE PRESS

P.O Box 1886
Kailua, HI 96734
slateridgepress@hawaii.rr.com

ISBN: 0982944411
ISBN-13: 9780982944417

First published by Island Heritage 2004
Slate Ridge Press edition 2011

Murder on Moloka'i © Chip Hughes 2004
"The Making of *Murder on Moloka'i*" © Chip Hughes 2011

For Stu Hilt,

Honolulu P.I.

ACKNOWLEDGEMENTS

Many thanks to my wife, Charlene Avallone, for her inspiration and editorial instinct, and to my mother, Kathryn Cooley Hughes, and to Stu Hilt for generously sharing his forty years' experience as a Honolulu P.I.

Specialist editors who assisted include Ku'ualoha Ho'omanawanui and Puhi Adams, Hawaiian language and culture; Rodney Morales, pidgin dialect; Scott Burlington, Hawaiian spellings and place names; Steve and Donna Curry, surfing scenes; Peter Read Smith, Big Island topography; Dr. Max B. Smith, mule behavior; Karen Roeller and Dr. Bani H. Win, medical examiner's procedures, Dr. Randy Baselt, blood work.

Thanks to Lorna Hershinow, Laurie Tomchak, and my Mānoa writing group: LaRene Despain, John Griffin, Linda Walters-Page, Sue Cowing, and Felix Smith. And to Buddy Bess, Bennett Hymer, Roger Jellinek, Eden-Lee Murray, and Ian MacMillan for their help; and to virtuoso with piano and pen, Les Peetz.

Special thanks to John Michener at Mediaspring for the Surfing Detective website, and to Island Heritage CEO Dale Madden and Art Director Scott Kaneshiro for the series logo and cover art.

Finally, a big *mahalo* to my invaluable editor Kirsten Whatley.

'A'ole kānā wai ma kēia wahi.

In this place there is no law.

one

"Mr. Cooke?" The throaty voice came through my office door in deep, honeyed tones that told me this was a woman I wanted to meet.

"Be right there." I slipped on some holey Levi's over my wet skin and groped in vain for a T-shirt, cursing myself for having gone surfing so close to a client appointment.

I opened the door to a tall, slim woman in her mid-twenties with chestnut hair and eyes the cool blue-grey of a glacier. Tommy Woo, my attorney, who had referred her, was right. I was "damn glad" this woman had come to see me, even if all I could remember was that she lived in Boston.

"Mr. Cooke . . . ?" She asked again in those rich tones, her brow furrowing as her eyes fell on the crescent of pink welts on my chest. *Tiger shark. Laniākea.*

She turned away.

I wrapped my damp beach towel around my shoulders. "Sorry, I . . . lost my shirt."

"I'm looking for Mr. Cooke, the private detective." She tried again.

"You are Miss . . . ?"

"Ridgely. Adrienne Ridgely."

I gestured to the Naugahyde chair by my desk and she sat. Her fruity perfume soon replaced the sharp odors wafting up from Maunakea Street below.

"I'm Mr. Cooke. Call me Kai."

She surveyed my soaked board shorts atop an expanding puddle of sea water on the dusty linoleum and then said without much conviction, "Mr. Woo told me you are the best detective in Honolulu."

"That was generous of him." I glanced down at my towel. "The reason I'm dressed this way is . . ."

She cut me off. "Nothing but the best for Sara. That's what I told Mr. Woo."

"And Sara is . . . ?"

"My sister."

"Why don't you tell me about her." I pulled a yellow legal pad from the jumble on my desk and found a pen.

"We were very close." Adrienne blinked her cool grey eyes and I wondered if she were about to cry. "Sara was the best sister I could ever have."

I jotted on the legal pad.

"She was always good to Mother and Father when they were alive. And she was good to me. She left me everything."

"She must have been a fine person."

"Sara was an attorney, you know." Adrienne said this as if I *should* know. "And a gifted teacher. And then there were her causes. She gave unselfishly to those causes."

"What happened to your sister?"

From a Louis Vuitton handbag of soft calf's leather she pulled a tissue. "Sara was only thirty-two."

"When she died?"

"Yes, in that horrible way." She worked the tissue with her fingers. "She fell off a cliff . . ."

I jotted on my pad.

"From a mule," she said.

"On Moloka'i?" Her story was beginning to sound familiar.

"Yes, they said it was an accident. But from the beginning I had my doubts."

"I remember now. I read a tribute to your sister in the *Advertiser* a while back."

Sara Ridgely-Parke had had a freak accident on Moloka'i. Ascending the switchback trail above the former leper colony at Kalaupapa, her mule had stumbled and catapulted her down the face of a thousand-foot cliff. She had been killed instantly. The newspaper had called the Harvard-trained attorney an "ecofeminist" committed to preserving the *'āina,* as Hawaiians call the land. I had seen her once in action at a rally to save a pristine surfing spot called Coconut Beach from a proposed strip mall. The fiery, strawberry-haired woman had galvanized me—and the crowd.

"Sara Ridgely-Parke." I jotted her name on my yellow pad. "So you want me to investigate the mule tour company?"

"No." Her voice lowered. "I have no intention of suing the tour company."

"Then why did Tommy send you?"

"I'm not here about money. I want justice."

I nodded, unsure how to reply.

"Sara was the first person ever to die on the Moloka'i mule tour. But she was no novice. We used to ride horses together in Brookline."

"Her experience with horses probably didn't matter,' I said. "There's nothing to riding a mule. You just sit there and the animal does the rest."

"Sara wouldn't fall from a mule," she insisted. "Anyway, I'm told those surefooted animals rarely stumble."

"Didn't the newspaper say the mule broke its leg?"

"I don't believe it." Adrienne fixed her teary eyes on me. "My sister was murdered."

"Murdered? By who?" I was starting to think she had an overactive imagination.

"Her ex-husband. J. Gregory Parke."

"Why would her ex want to kill her?"

"Sara received half of their home in the divorce." She daubed away a tear. "It's an oceanfront estate in Kāhala. Worth a fortune. Greg wouldn't part with the place, so he had to pay her off."

"How much did she get?"

"After lawyers' fees, about four million."

"Parke had that kind of cash?"

She shrugged. "He's a developer."

"Your environmentalist sister married a developer? That's hard to imagine."

"I never understood what she saw in him. We didn't always have such different taste in men."

"So you think Parke was so angry after forking out all that money that he killed your sister?"

"Yes." Her lower lip quivered.

"Do you have any evidence?" I was sympathetic, but still skeptical.

"Greg abused her during their marriage. It all came out in the hearing. And after the divorce he wouldn't leave her alone. I think he finally just boiled over."

"Wait a minute." I stopped writing on my pad. "Your sister fell from a mule on Moloka'i. How could Parke have been responsible?"

"I don't know." She crushed her damp tissue into a little ball. "I just know he was."

"Was Parke on Moloka'i when the accident happened?"

"That's why I'm hiring you. To find out."

"I'll have to fly to Moloka'i. My regular hourly rate, plus three hundred a day for neighbor island travel."

"Cost doesn't matter. I'm doing this for Sara."

"O.K. I'll start with the tour company, then check out the accident scene and interview witnesses. After that I can give you a better idea if you have a case. For the initial investigation I'll need a two thousand dollar retainer."

She didn't even blink, just pulled out her checkbook. Her tears were gone now. "Will my Boston check be all right?"

"Sure. Where are you staying?"

"The Halekūlani."

"Can I give you a lift back to Waikīkī?"

Her blue-grey eyes took on a touch of frost. "My cab is waiting in the alley behind the flower shop." She was referring to Fujiyama's Flower Leis, on the ground floor below my office.

"I'll call you as soon as I have anything to report," I said, reaching for my wallet. "And here's my card."

She glanced at the sand-toned card that said "Surfing Detective" and "Confidential Investigations–All Islands." Above these words was a full-color longboard rider with toes on the nose: back gracefully arched, knees bent slightly, arms outstretched like wings, turquoise wave curling over board and surfer alike. A thing of beauty.

Unfortunately, my card failed to make much of an impression on her. Her expression didn't change.

"You might be surprised by the crank calls I get." I tried to lighten the moment. "Just the other day this wacko phones for Jack Lord. 'Book 'em, Danno!' the guy says, delusional from watching reruns of 'Hawaii Five-O,' I guess."

"Interesting." Adrienne rose and edged toward the door.

"And then a few weeks back," I continued, on a roll now, "some woman with a breathy voice whispers into my phone, *'Thomas Magnum?'* Before I can break the news that her heartthrob Tom Selleck left the islands, she hangs up. Crazy, huh?"

"Call me if you need more money." Adrienne abruptly stepped from my office. I watched her silky dress sway like an undulating wave as she glided down the stairs.

A moment later I gazed down onto Maunakea Street and saw a taxi pull in front of the flower shop. Adrienne climbed in and glanced up at me with those cool eyes.

Suddenly I felt a rare chill in the tropic air.

two

Later that day I flew to Moloka'i. It was Wednesday and turbulent for early October. Squeezed into a propeller-driven Twin-Otter airplane, slightly larger than my car, I had my first leisure to think about the bizarre events that had sent me on this impromptu jaunt.

So far there were only questions and none of them added up to what I'd call a case. Instead, there was a death by falling from a mule, which could be nothing more than an accident. But the victim's sister was crying murder. And she had pointed the finger at Sara's ex-husband—J. Gregory Parke. This seemed unlikely. Unless media accounts of the accident had been totally wrong.

Was I bound for Moloka'i on a fool's errand? Maybe. But at least I was getting paid.

I tried to get comfortable in my tiny seat and opened up the afternoon *Star-Bulletin*. On the front page of the business section was an artist's sketch of a proposed Moloka'i resort called Kalaupapa Cliffs. Brainchild of Umbro Zia, a shadowy Indonesian developer, and the islands' largest private landholder, Chancellor Trust, Kalaupapa Cliffs promised to loom grand

and blindingly white. It resembled an art deco Taj Mahal with marble spas and meandering pools and hundreds of ocean-view suites—another luxury palace for the super rich.

Evidently, a technicality concerning the building site was holding up construction. Its fate awaited a vote of the Land Zoning Board. Considering the clout of the Chancellor Trust, the outcome was hardly in doubt.

The Twin-Otter rattled along, barely above the Honolulu skyline. The Aloha Tower drifted by, then the ivory crescent of Waikīkī Beach. Longboards floated below on the turquoise sea like pastel toothpicks. Outrigger canoes etched frothy trails through the rolling surf.

Soon we left Oʻahu behind and below us lay wind-whipped Kaʻiwi Channel—the twenty-five miles of whitecaps between Oʻahu and Molokaʻi. The tiny plane bumped along as if plowing through the choppy swells beneath us. Between jolts I folded my newspaper and took out some clippings I had gathered on the subject of my dubious case.

The obituary photo showed Sara Ridgely-Parke to be the striking, youthful woman I remembered so vividly from the rally. Her eyes had the same flinty quality as Adrienne's, though with an emerald tint.

A Harvard-trained attorney who taught environmental law at the University of Hawaiʻi, Sara had crusaded for affordable housing and "green" stewardship of the islands. Her greatest victory had been the Save Coconut Beach initiative, in which she and other activists saved the pristine windward surfing spot from development.

From the news coverage at the time, I remembered that developers and conservative politicians alike despised Sara's "ecofeminist" views. Being both an environmentalist and a feminist put her at the very radical end of the spectrum in their eyes. The article went on with lavish praise from Professor Rush McWhorter, Sara's law school adversary and legal counsel for the Chancellor Trust. "A tragic loss to the people of Hawai'i," his quote read, which seemed at odds with the public rancor between the two during her life.

Another jolt of turbulence shook the Twin-Otter. I set down the obituary and picked up a wedding clipping.

After her Coconut Beach victory, Sara had become the darling of local environmentalists. Yet she then married developer J. Gregory Parke, a bald blimp of a man twenty years her senior, and lived with him in the ritziest neighborhood in the Hawaiian Islands.

What an odd couple! Their contentious divorce seemed predictable given their strange conflict of interests. I tucked the clips back into my briefcase and peered down at the inky whitecaps below. Sara's short and admirable life had had its contradictions, as I suppose all lives do. But could these contradictions have any bearing on the fatal stumble of a mule?

It was a stretch to think so. A long stretch.

Our first sighting of Moloka'i revealed the West End's pristine Pāpōhaku Beach, a three-mile ribbon of frothing surf and golden sand. One of the longest, most stunning beaches in the islands, it's remote and often deserted. I saw not one surfer, swimmer, or sunbather.

This dramatic beach, and most of Moloka'i, has escaped the urban sprawl so prevalent on the other islands because residents here, primarily Hawaiian, have rallied repeatedly against unwanted development. Though jobs have been scarce since Moloka'i's pineapple plantations closed, forcing more and more *kama'āina* to scramble for a living, few long-time residents see Waikīkī-style resorts on their unspoiled island as the answer.

The Twin-Otter angled and crossed over the island's arid West End. From previous visits, I recognized the rugged terrain. Sloping plateaus painted the west in cocoa brown and rust red; sheer sea cliffs in the east soared in moss green. The thirty-eight-mile island pointed east like an index finger with one small irregularity—a bump on the north side where the middle knuckle would be. This knuckle was my ultimate destination: Kalaupapa. The once-infamous leper colony, now a national park, sat on a small peninsula beneath the world's tallest sea cliffs. It was from these cliffs that Sara Ridgely-Parke had plunged.

In Honolulu, I had obtained the medical examiner's report on Sara's autopsy. It offered little new information. I had also phoned the mule tour company and learned there was a log of all riders, including the four others in Sara's party. A guide named Johnny Kaluna had agreed to walk me down the cliff trail to the site of the accident, then on to Kalaupapa. I arranged to meet him at seven thirty the next morning.

The Twin-Otter began its bumpy descent as we passed over red dirt fields, inhabited by stunted *kiawe* and grazing cattle. Only one thread-thin highway, devoid of cars, gave evidence of civilization. A few other rusty side roads branched off from the highway. But I saw no vehicles there either.

Once in my rented car, I turned east onto a two-lane blacktop that wandered over terrain as red and rugged as I had seen from the air. With a blood-orange sun sinking behind me, I headed toward my motel in Kaunakakai and continued wrestling with the case.

I tried to imagine a disgruntled ex-husband wanting to kill his former wife, a wealthy developer who felt cheated out of more money than I could make in a lifetime. But J. Gregory Parke had far more to lose than money if he got caught as a murderer. And surely he could not hope to get away with murder when he and Sara were so in the public eye. Unless he could make murder look like an accident.

But how could even a millionaire arrange for a mule to break its leg halfway up the Kalaupapa trail?

I suspected Adrienne Ridgely was grasping at straws. She was grieving the loss of her sister and needed to do something to make herself feel that justice had been served. It was unlikely that the facts I had would add up to murder, but I planned to work hard to earn her retainer. I would follow every lead until either the trail turned cold or her money ran out. Then it dawned on me. With Adrienne's sizable inheritance, her money would never run out.

On the way to my motel, I drove through Moloka'i's commercial hub, Kaunakakai—three short blocks of ramshackle shops with tin roofs and hitching posts for horses and mules. The familiar signs rolled by: Kanemitsu Bakery ("Home of Moloka'i sweet bread"), Friendly Isle Market, Moloka'i Fish and Dive, Sun Whole Foods.

An old yellow dog with a hoary white muzzle ambled in front of my car. I braked. Though I should have expected him. This ghost-like retriever has been hanging out by the pumps at Kalama's service station for years. His slow gait takes him across the main street each day, to the lawn of the public library, where he curls up in the shade for a snooze. The fact that this old yellow dog has survived so long says volumes about Kaunakakai.

One block *makai,* on the ocean side of town, I checked into my "deluxe" oceanfront cottage, more expensive than the 'Ukulele Inn's other rooms because it was farthest from the notoriously lively Banyan Tree Bar. But my digs were still rustic— a shack really, without TV or phone, but with a beachside *lānai* just wide enough for two plastic lawn chairs.

At sunset I sat in one of these chairs and peered across the mango-tinted water at the humpbacked island of Lāna'i. Farther in the amber distance lay Maui, whose twin peaks resembled the sea-kissed breasts of a reclining goddess.

As night fell, I decided to investigate the sweet strains of Hawaiian music coming from the Banyan Tree Bar. A three-piece band was crowded onto the tiny stage, strumming and singing my favorite song about Moloka'i:

> *Take me back . . . take me back . . .*
> *Back to da kine.*
> *All over, mo' bettah,*
> *Moloka'i. I will return.* [1]

I stepped up to the bar and ordered a beer. The bartender, a Hawaiian guy about my age, mid-thirties, turned out to be a surfer. We hit it off right away. As he pulled the tap, then slid a frothy mug across the bar, we began "talking story" above the sweet sounds coming from the band.

---

[1] Song lyrics from "Moloka'i Slide" written by Larry Helm and first recorded in 1997 by Ehukai.

I'm not Hawaiian, but I can talk like one local when the situation calls for it. I was *hānaied*, or adopted, when I was eight by the Kealoha *'ohana,* a Hawaiian family related to me through my aunt's marriage. Because of that, most Hawaiians I meet don't consider me *haole,* but just another guy who loves the beauty of the *'āina* and the surf as much as they do.

The bartender and I talked about Moloka'i's uncrowded breaks and the effects of commercialization on surfing. From my wallet I reached for a ten, setting it on the bar under my two-dollar mug. My newfound friend glanced at the green bill.

"Heard anyt'ing 'bout dat *haole* lady," I asked off-handedly, "who wen' fall off da Kalaupapa cliff one mont' ago?"

"She one lawyer or somet'ing?" he replied.

"Dat's her."

"Nah," the bartender said. "At first ev'rybody talk—'good-looking *wahine'*—and dat kine stuffs, but aftah da accident I nevah hear nut'ing."

"Da Hawai'i Tourism Board like hush 'um up? Bad fo' business, eh?"

"Dunno, brah. Maybe dey t'ink so."

I stood up to go, leaving my ten on the bar.

"T'anks, eh?" the bartender again eyed the bill.

"No mention." I started for my room. "Maybe see you laytah."

The Hawaiian music faded as I walked across the grass lawn. This conversation had cost me a few bucks and yielded little of immediate value. But that wasn't the point. If ever I needed information on anyone at the 'Ukulele Inn, or anywhere on Moloka'i, I felt sure I could count on my new *bruddah.*

Later that evening, I climbed into bed and reviewed the medical examiner's report again. Cut and dried. Sara had the fractures and internal injuries anyone might receive from a long fall. No sign of foul play. No traces of drugs or medications.

I needed more to go on. Maybe tomorrow's mule ride would reveal something I was overlooking, something to give me reason to believe that Adrienne Ridgely was not deluding herself. I listened to the faint sounds of the Hawaiian band as I switched off the light.

three

"Errr-Errr-Eroooo! Errr-Eroooooo!"

A rooster strutting the grounds of the 'Ukulele Inn jolted me awake the next morning before dawn.

I slipped on some makeshift hiking clothes and drove into Kaunakakai. At Kanemitsu Bakery I ate some Moloka'i French toast and ordered a take-out coffee before heading for the cliffs of Kalaupapa.

The narrow highway hugged the arid shoreline, then climbed north through miles of open land. The rugged desert-like plateau of the West End soon transformed into upland mountains and emerald forests. The air grew cool. The higher the curving road climbed, the lusher the canopy of green.

At the highway's summit, my windshield clouded with mist. I cranked on the wipers, but the mist kept obscuring the glass like steam on a shower door.

Across from the ridge overlooking the former leper colony, I spotted the mule pack station. Guided Mule Tours read the sign. The Western-style lettering above the red clapboards and a rusty tin roof looked right out of a cowboy movie. An empty corral choked with grass suggested no mules had been there for a while.

I pulled up in front of the barn and went in search of the guide I was supposed to meet. Inside was a small office with not much more than a water cooler, Coke machine, and display of T-shirts for sale that said: "I'd Rather Be Riding a Mule on Moloka'i." Beyond the office was a tack room and stable containing wooden feeding troughs, rubbed smooth and shiny by the mules' muzzles. But no animals.

"Johnny Kaluna?" My voice echoed off the clapboards.

My watch said seven thirty. The time of our appointment. Maybe he operated on Hawaiian time—that leisurely island pace that pays little attention to the hands of a clock? Then I heard the approach of a rattling vehicle. An old Jeep pickup appeared on the ridge, bed piled high with yellow bales of hay.

A wiry *hapa*-Hawaiian in a black felt cowboy hat climbed down from the truck. His mustache was flecked with silver and his face tanned reddish-brown like *koa*. The fine lines around his eyes and deep creases of his smile suggested he was more than sixty. His jeans were worn white at the thighs—not fashionably faded, but really worn. A pair of scuffed and muddied boots and a red *palaka*, or checkered Western shirt, rounded out his rugged appearance.

This man was a *paniolo*—a Hawaiian cowboy.

We stood in the mist and introduced ourselves. The guide's deeply tanned face wore an expression of dignity, softened somewhat by his easy smile.

"Call me Kaluna, eh?" He spoke in pidgin, extending his right hand. "Eve'body does."

"Kaluna, where da mules?" I replied in kind and shook his hand by hooking thumbs, island style.

"West Moloka'i Ranch, waiting fo' lawyers to draw up new papahs."

"What papahs?" I studied the *paniolo's* lively brown eyes.

"New liability waiver for customahs to sign. Eva since da accident we suspend da tour." The guide eyed me warily. "Kai, you one lawyer?"

"Private investigator." I handed him my card.

"Detective, eh?" He eyed the full-color wave rider. "And surfah too?"

I nodded. "No worry, my client no like sue da tour company."

"*Hū!*" Kaluna let out a big breath. "Not much work while da stable shut down, except driving to da ranch and feeding da mules."

"Kaluna, you like tell me 'bout da accident?"

The mule guide's smile faded. "Was worst day of my life." He paused to reflect, his expression turning more somber. "Da *wahine,* Sara, she wen' fall 'bout one t'ousand feet down da *pali.* Was one doctor in da party, but he no could do nut'ing—fo' da *wahine* or fo' Coco."

"Who Coco?"

"Da mule, bruddah." Kaluna's brown eyes glistened. "Good mule. Not like Coco fo' stumble. I bury him wit' one backhoe by da trailhead. You see da grave when we hike down."

"You bury da mule yourself?" I wondered at such trouble and expense for a pack animal.

"Was my favorite." The guide spoke slowly, holding back emotion. "I had one tour helicopter hoist 'em up da trail." Kaluna motioned me toward the barn. "Ovah hea. I get you da doctor's name and da oddahs."

We walked into the office. From a drawer behind the counter Kaluna pulled a guest book of black leatherette with silver trim. He opened to Wednesday, September 6.

"Dis' da day. Slow day. Was only four riders besides da *wahine,* Sara. All come separate. One was da doctor. And two more *kāne* and anoddah *wahine.*"

"Three men and one woman?"

He nodded.

"O.K. if I take picture of da four names?"

"Whatevahs." He handed me the dusty black book. The doctor, Benjamin Goto, lived in Honolulu. The second man, Milton Yu, gave an address on the Hāmākua Coast of the Big Island. The third, Emery Archibald, listed only "Island Fantasy Holidays, Glendale, CA." And the woman, Heather Linborg, lived on Maui. With the 35-millimeter camera I always carry along on cases, an old but dependable Olympus, I photographed the relevant pages of the book.

"What you remembah 'bout da four people?" I asked.

"Was one mont' ago," Kaluna replied. "Usually forget after dat long, but da accident, you know, stay *pa'a* in my mind."

"No can blame you, bruddah." I encouraged him.

"Da oddah *wahine,* Heather—*hū!*—was one nice-looking *pua.* Young flower, yeah? Blonde kine." He winked. "If only I one handsome young *kāne* again!"

"Da blonde *wahine* wen' talk with Sara?"

"Nah, Heather wen' talk mo' wit' da local *Pāk□* guy, Milton Yu."

"How 'bout dis Archibald? He wen' talk with Sara or act funny kine around her?"

"He talk wit' her. But no diff'rent from anybody else. Jus', you know, talk story kine."

"And da doctor?"

"Same t'ing. Dat doctor was *momona.* Fat, plenny fat. I give him my biggest mule, *Ikaika.* Means strong, you know."

"Did da doctor help Sara when she wen' fall?"

"No use," the mule guide continued. "Da *pali* too steep. No can reach her."

I pulled out the photo Adrienne had given me of Parke and showed it to Kaluna. "Evah see dis guy?"

Kaluna's brown eyes squinted. He twitched his silvery mustache. "'*Ae,* I seen him."

"You have?" I tried not to show my surprise.

"On da mule ride to Kalaupapa—one, maybe two days befo' da accident."

"Can prove dat?"

"By da guest book." He turned the dusty book back one page to the day before Sara's fatal ride. Sure enough, on the list was "J. G. Parke." Could Adrienne be right after all?

"You remembah anyt'ing 'bout Parke?"

"Not much. Was quiet. He nevah take no interest in da tour."

I put away the photo, still trying to cover my surprise. "O.K. We hike down da trail now to see where da *wahine* fall?"

He nodded and took out a cash box. "You wanna pay now or laytah?"

"Now is fine." From my wallet I handed him some bills.

"I no like ask, but no paying customahs since da accident."

"Nah, no worry."

We trekked on foot toward the cliffs. Although I was still unsure what I was hoping to find, Kaluna's registry with Parke's name in it had made me hyper-alert.

To reach the trailhead, we hiked through some ironwoods, then down a curving path sprinkled with mule droppings and rotting guava, whose pink meat lured clouds of fruit flies. The air was ripe. All along the path were warning signs: *Kapu:* Unauthorized Persons Keep Out.

The mist that had fogged my windshield suddenly descended, as we approached the trailhead. Wind whistled through a stand of ironwoods at the cliff's edge. On the precipice overlooking Kalaupapa stood a crude wooden cross inscribed, "Coco."

"Carve dat myself . . ." Kaluna said softly.

"Coco' one special mule." I consoled the *paniolo* as I glanced down toward the peninsula below—a steep fall indeed, and one from which not even a veteran horse rider could expect to survive.

four

The Kaluapapa trail began like a stroll in the park, wide and gently sloping. But soon the path narrowed, descending over rain-slick boulders, potholes dug by mule hoofs, and red mud.

At the first opportunity, I peeked over the *pali* and gazed down again nearly two thousand feet to Kalaupapa. Wild seas from the north pounded its craggy shore. Wind-whipped mists drove slantwise across the salt-bitten land, gathering like gauze against the towering sea cliffs. Their rocky faces rose like prison walls from the boiling surf.

Awesome beauty. Stark desolation. Fierce, unforgiving nature. No wonder this forbidding peninsula had once been called a living tomb. No wonder I suddenly felt bleak again about my long shot case.

We passed a gate posted with a more severe warning than the first *Kapu* signs: Hawai'i Law Forbids Entry Beyond This Point Without Written Permission.

Kaluna explained that access to the colony had been strictly controlled before sulfone drugs rendered leprosy, known today as Hansen's disease, non-contagious. The *pali* trail first opened in 1889, the year the colony's most celebrated savior,

Father Damien, died. For many years after, the three miles and twenty-six switchbacks were traversed mostly by pack mules ferrying supplies to the victims below. The savvy mules could pick their own way down the sixteen-hundred-foot cliff without a human guide, and likewise return. So it was nothing for mules in modern times to carry tourists safely on thousands of trips. That is, until Sara Ridgely-Parke's fall.

Why had Sara come here? Was her trip connected in some way to her ecological passion, or her desire to evade her ex-husband's constant hounding? Did she perhaps feel affinity for the sufferers of Kalaupapa—victims of rape and sodomy and murder, not to mention starvation?

'A'ole kānā wai ma kēia wahi had been the cry of leprosy victims. "In this place there is no law."

The first official switchback in the trail—marked by a big red "1"—brought a cool, shady corner canopied by trees. No slippery rocks. No outrageous drop. Not even a view. Therefore, not likely the turn where Sara had fallen.

Before reaching the second switchback we passed yet another warning: Stop! Go Back Unless You Have Written Permit. We hiked on.

The red numeral announcing switchback three brought a dramatic view of Kalaupapa, and a difficult section of trail. Kaluna picked up the pace. I kept my eyes glued to my feet.

Halfway down the *pali,* at switchback thirteen, we heard the first faint rumblings of surf. Beyond this hairpin turn, boulders lay in the trail above a sheer drop. Kaluna stopped suddenly and glanced up.

"Wish I had da money Chancellor Trust gonna make on dat development." He pointed to a ridge towering over us.

"Development?" I said. "But dis national park land, yeah?"

"'Ae, jus' to da *pali,* but Chancellor own da conservation lan' beyond dat." Kaluna scratched his silver-flecked mustache. "Dey own da lan' and da politicians too!"

"What Chancellor going to build up there?"

"'Kalaupapa Cliffs'—hotel, condos, spas. All dat kine stuffs."

"Now I remembah." I linked the development to yesterday's *Star-Bulletin.*

"When da last leprosy patient pass on, Kalaupapa be one busy kine national park. Da tourist flock hea . . ." Kaluna paused. "Chancellor make plenny *kālā*—plenny money."

"Good fo' your business? More mule riders?"

"Maybe, but I no like condos up on da cliff."

I nodded in agreement.

"Anyway, jus' 'round da next bend where da *wahine* fall."

We turned a sharp left at switchback fifteen and gazed down the pocked, boulder-strewn track—a treacherous-looking patch. The wicked combination of jagged boulders and pitched steps was apparently the best the trailblazers who chiseled this rocky path could do. My knees involuntarily trembled as I listened to the waves lapping the shore a thousand feet below. We could see the beach clearly now: milk-chocolate sand, ultramarine swells, sparkling white foam. No guard rails obstructed the view.

If a four-hoofed animal were prone to stumble anywhere on the trail, this would be the place. Kaluna must have read my mind.

"Da *wahine* ride Coco up da trail toward da bend." He pointed to the red "15." "I take da lead and she ride near da back." Kaluna paused. "Den hear Coco bray and da *wahine* scream. Dat's all. I no can see her fall."

"You spot her down below? Or hear more screams?"

"Nah." Kaluna shook his head, a tortured look on his face. "No can do nut'ing. I call to her. Da oddahs do too. But no use."

"What happen' den?"

"Since no can do nut'ing, I took da oddahs to da top and call da police. They wen' send one helicopter. Meantime, I take my rifle back down to Coco. He still lying dere on da path, peaceful kine. Look at me wit' big brown eyes and I say, 'You been one good mule, Coco.' Den I do what I gotta do."

"Sorry, bruddah."

"T'anks. Den da helicopter pick da *wahine* off da *pali,* fly her to O'ahu. But too late."

"About dis Parke guy." I tried to make a connection. "He 'round here da day of da accident?"

"I no remembah seeing him." The mule guide shrugged.

I took some photos, then searched around the site for evidence but found nothing. During the month since Sara's death the trail had been washed by rains, blown by gusty trade winds, and scorched by the sun. The winds alone would have carried away anything not bolted down.

If Parke was behind Sara's fall, he had left no evidence here. But that probably wasn't going to change my client's mind. Adrienne seemed hell-bent on her murder theory and might never stop believing it—unless my investigation proved otherwise.

five

Just before switchback sixteen, a sharp jackknife turn, I noticed a flat-topped boulder beside the trail. On top of it stood a makeshift shrine of religious figurines—Madonna, baby Jesus, turbaned wise men—encircled by a dried *maile lei* and rosary beads. A wilted red rose lay beside this somber, huddled group. And a fresh rose lay next to it. The roses struck me as odd amidst these rugged surroundings.

Had some adoring admirer fondly remembered Sara Ridgely-Parke on this remote stretch of trail? Someone who was feeling pain at her loss? Red roses, I imagined, were not that easy to come by in this remote part of Moloka'i. Who cared that much for Sara?

As we passed, Kaluna quickly crossed himself, making me wonder how long the shrine had been here. Before I could ask, the old *paniolo* abruptly launched into a homespun speech about Kalaupapa, sounding like he'd given it hundreds of times before.

The peninsula, he began in a tour guide voice, was first settled by Hawaiians in about 1000 AD. The small spit of land had been a fishing and agricultural village until 1868, when

King Kamehameha V sent the first boatload of leprosy patients to be quarantined there.

Leprosy at the time was misunderstood and greatly feared, much as AIDS is today. Boat captains tossed helpless victims overboard to swim ashore. Those who drowned were the lucky ones. Those who didn't had to fend for themselves on the isolated peninsula. Their average survival rate was about two years.

Kaluna explained that there was little to support patients here: no dependable food supply, shelter, clothing, or medicine. Helpers called *kōkua* were permitted at first, but soon forbidden. Victims remained utterly alone, without family or friends. Kalaupapa became known as "the place where one is buried alive." No wonder people dreaded being diagnosed and sent here.

I wasn't surprised that Father Damien, now a candidate for sainthood, was not uniformly appreciated during his life, especially by the State Board of Health. He took under his care seven to eight hundred leprosy patients, whose number eventually grew to as many as thirteen hundred. Now, Kaluna said, only about fifty residents remained—of their own free will— and most were growing old. He said they stayed for various reasons, some from their attachment to the only home they have ever known.

At nine that morning we finally reached sea level. The quiet village of Kalaupapa lay another quarter mile to the east. The path to the village wove above the deserted beach we had seen from the cliffs, a gorgeous, wide beach lined with stately ironwoods whose needles padded the trail. No one swam. No one surfed. No one beach walked. It seemed a shame. As we drew nearer, we saw the expected warning: Stop! Entry Pass Violators Subject to Citation.

In the village, a young woman in a park service uniform introduced herself as our official guide. Haunani offered us a tour in her Jeep, and I began to wonder what I was looking for here as we passed Kalaupapa's simple amenities: a one-pump gas station, a small general store, a souvenir shop in a converted Buddhist temple, a carpenter's shop, a government motor pool, an invitation-only guest house dubbed the "Kalaupapa Sheraton," a pier for the biannual barges that ferried heavy supplies, three churches, and seven thousand graves. Mostly unmarked.

If Kaunakakai was a slow town, Kalaupapa was frozen in time. I watched as a half dozen axis deer roamed the village like pets, grazing on cottage lawns. The cottages looked empty, but Haunani explained that residents seldom showed themselves among strangers. There was a deafening silence to Kalauapapa. The only sound beyond the surf was the whispering fronds of lonely palms.

Haunani said she remembered Sara's striking appearance from her visit to the colony. And when I showed our guide the photo of Parke, she recognized him as well. After a full month she still recalled his grim, determined face, so unlike other visitors' expressions of curiosity and wonder. What had Parke had on his mind?

The return hike up the *pali* to "topside" Moloka'i took about an hour and a quarter. We didn't push. Kaluna let me lead. I'm fairly sure I slowed him down. But he patiently stayed behind me, step for step. Despite my conditioning from surfing, my chest heaved and my heart drummed. Sweat stung my eyes.

My thighs burned. At least the steady climb allowed me to comb the trail again for clues to Sara's mysterious death. But no clues did I find.

We finally reached the top at half past eleven. As I drove back to the 'Ukulele Inn, I reluctantly admitted to myself that Adrienne's hunch about Parke might have some basis in fact. His mere presence at Kalaupapa near the time of Sara's death seemed more than a coincidence. I itched to interview Parke immediately upon return to Honolulu. But those were my emotions talking, not my head. I knew the best course would be to gather information about him first, since he might not consent to see me more than once, if at all.

I collected my things from the beach cottage and checked out at quarter to one—nearly an hour late, but still in time to catch my flight. Before long another Twin-Otter was winging me back to O'ahu. I was too preoccupied with questions about the case to pay much attention to the bumpy ride.

My trip to Moloka'i had served more to increase the mystery surrounding Sara's death rather than to solve it.

six

The flower *lei* shop beneath my office is the perfect buffer between me and the pungent aromas of Chinatown below. And it offers my clients a degree of anonymity. They can linger among the perfumy *lei*, then slip unnoticed up the orange shag stairs. Even if detected, they can pretend to be patronizing one of the four other tenants of Mrs. Fujiyama's building, a decaying pre-war specimen ornamented with two-headed dragons, serpents, wild boars, and Chinese characters in red.

Inside the flower shop today, Mrs. Fujiyama was ringing up a customer with a ginger *lei*. The ginger's sweet, pungent odor raised the hair on the back of my neck.

"Good morning, Mrs. Fujiyama." I said as the customer departed.

Mrs. Fujiyama peered up at me knowingly over her half-glasses. "Ah, Mr. Cooke. One pretty young lady come see you. Bought tuberose and orchid *lei*."

"Adrienne?"

"Upstairs now. *Haole* lady. Very pretty!"

"Thanks for the tip." I smiled.

"Nice young lady for Mr. Cooke." Mrs. Fujiyama bowed graciously.

I climbed the stairs to the musty second floor and peered down the hallway toward the surfer airbrushed on my office door. Adrienne Ridgely stood by him statuesquely, clutching a *lei*. She looked transformed. The tropic sun had deepened the color in her cheeks and highlighted the reds and golds in her chestnut hair.

As I approached, Adrienne stretched her arms toward me and placed the *lei* around my neck. Her perfume, mixed with the intoxicating odor of the tuberose, drew me nearer. We touched. She abruptly stepped back. The blush heightened in her cheeks.

"Ah, what a surprise," I said, searching for more intelligent words. "Why the *lei*?"

"For taking my case." She quickly regained her composure. "My sister is finally going to get the justice she deserves."

"I'm not sure we have a case yet," I admitted. "Although I did discover something on Moloka'i yesterday."

I unlocked the two dead bolts and swung open the thick mahogany door. The tuberose *lei* instantly revived the stale air in my office. I opened my window and couldn't help but notice how gracefully Adrienne slid into my client chair. She glanced atop my filing cabinet at the tarnished trophy teetering there—Classic Longboard–Mākaha–Third Place–then turned her cool gaze back to me.

"So the big news is," I started, "your former brother-in-law rode to Kalaupapa the day before Sara died."

"He *did?*" Adrienne's eyes widened. She seemed even more surprised than I had been.

"The guide doesn't remember seeing Parke on the day of the accident, but said he acted preoccupied when he took the tour the previous day. His mind was apparently elsewhere."

"I know where it was," Adrienne said almost to herself, her expressive brow working again.

"It's going to take more than his mule ride to build a case against him," I said, trying to give her a sense of the magnitude of evidence needed to convict a man of murder. "We have a long way to go. But, fortunately, there were four witnesses besides the guide, Kaluna. I plan to interview each in person before confronting Parke. Their testimonies may give us more leverage against him."

"When will you start?" She looked at me hopefully.

"Today," I said. "The first witness is a doctor named Benjamin Goto who practices here in Honolulu. I lined up an interview for eleven o'clock. It should require little time and expense."

"Whatever it takes."

"Interviewing the other three may be more challenging. One lives on Maui, another on the rural Hāmākua Coast of the Big Island, and the last in a Los Angeles suburb. If you want to cut costs, I can try phone interviews, though I don't think they're nearly as effective."

"No," Adrienne agreed. "Interview each in person."

"Your retainer should still cover the trip to Maui. But I'll need another two thousand for travel to the Big Island and Los Angeles."

"Why don't I just write you a check now?" Adrienne reached into her calfskin purse. She was determined.

I took the crisp Boston check and tucked it into my top desk drawer. "I'll call you after the interview with Dr. Goto then."

Adrienne rose. The highlights in her hair caught the sunlight filtering through my window. "If anyone can undercover my sister's murder, I trust it's you."

"Thanks for the vote of confidence," I said, the intoxicating scent of the tuberose mixed with her fruity perfume starting to make me dizzy. "And for the *lei*."

She nodded and turned to go. I took the opportunity to escort her down the orange shag stairs. Mrs. Fujiyama smiled when she saw us together.

Outside the flower shop, Adrienne climbed into her waiting cab. The yellow sedan swept down Maunakea, past the lurid neon signs that glow day and night on Hotel Street.

seven

Before my meeting with Dr. Goto, I made some telephone inquiries about him. Benjamin Goto had practiced medicine on Kapiʻolani Boulevard for twelve years, I learned. His license was in good standing and only one minor complaint had been filed against him by a patient. Goto's field was infectious diseases. He had earned his medical degree in the Virgin Islands and spent one undergraduate year at the University of Hawaiʻi, where, before her untimely death, Sara had taught in the law school.

On my way to Dr. Goto's office, my Impala growled along Kapiʻolani, turning a few heads. I bought the teal blue ʻ69 Chevy with only fifty-two-thousand original miles. Its big V-8 engine was what hooked me, but equally important, the backseat was removable, so my longboard could slide right in.

The doctor's office was in a mirrored tower at 1555 Kapiʻolani near Ala Moana Shopping Center. Its lobby glinted with enough marble to sink the proverbial battleship. I rode the elevator to the eighteenth floor. A few minutes before eleven, I found a door with a polished brass plate: Benjamin Goto, M.D.

The posh waiting room contained the usual ferns, seascapes, and recent issues of *People, Good Housekeeping, Sports Illustrated, Honolulu,* and *Hawaii Business News.* A receptionist with a professional smile asked me to take a seat. Twenty minutes later—not bad for the medical profession—she sent me in.

Dr. Goto didn't appear at all like the rugged outdoor type, as I had expected, but was a paunchy and affable man, probably in his forties. His ample jowls and rounded belly reminded me of a contented Buddha. He greeted me with smiling dark eyes.

"Please be seated, Mr. Cooke." The doctor made a sweeping gesture with great formality.

"Call me Kai." I wanted to put us on more friendly terms.

"Ben Goto." He offered me his hand and we shook.

The doctor moved behind his spacious teak desk and directed me toward a matching chair. His medical degrees and certificates hung on the wall, along with a photo of Caesar's Palace in Las Vegas—a slimmer Dr. Goto standing proudly before the glittering casino with a black-suited man in dark glasses.

"That's a handsome picture of you." I pointed to the Vegas photo.

Dr. Goto grinned. "Ah, yes, my salad days," he quipped. "Shakespeare, don't you know?"

I wondered why the younger Goto would be in Nevada with a character dressed like a mafioso.

"Thank you for seeing me on such short notice, Dr. Goto. My client appreciates your willingness to talk about Sara Ridgely-Parke's death."

"Such a pity." The doctor rocked back, his belly protruding from his white coat. He spoke in precise, proper English. "She seemed a remarkably intelligent woman."

"Apparently she was."

"I regret that I could not render medical treatment, but she was simply inaccessible."

"The mule guide confirms that. Neither he nor the police fault you."

"Still, it was most vexing." He frowned. "I could do nothing, don't you see. Absolutely nothing."

"May I ask where you were when Sara fell?"

"Certainly . . ." Dr. Goto paused to gather his thoughts. "I rode at the front of the party, immediately behind the guide. Ms. Ridgely-Parke rode near the back."

"Did you see her fall?"

"I am afraid not. Though her scream was chilling enough."

"You saw nothing?"

"The accident happened quite quickly, Mr. Cooke. By the time I turned around, it was over."

"Was there any warning, any indication of something wrong before she fell?"

"Not that I recall. It was a tricky section of trail–steep and rocky–but other sections had also been rough."

"Did you know the victim before that day on Moloka'i?"

"I had heard of her, of course. During the Save Coconut Beach initiative one could hardly pick up a newspaper or turn on the television without seeing her youthful face."

"Did you have any particular opinion about her? Or about her political activities?"

"I admired her. That's why it is such a pity to lose her. Legions of people mouth pieties about protecting the environment, but how many willingly endanger themselves to further the cause?"

"If you don't mind me asking, why did you go to Kalaupapa?"

"I don't mind at all." Dr. Goto smiled with Buddha-like serenity. "I am a specialist in infectious diseases. Kalaupapa offers a rare opportunity to study Hansen's disease patients. They could come to my Honolulu office, of course. But I wanted to see them first in their own habitat."

"Had you been to Kalaupapa before?"

"Actually, no." He gazed at me placidly. "But I had always desired to go."

"Why didn't you before?"

"One thing leads to another. Time goes by." He managed two clichés in one breath.

"Did you study any patients at Kalaupapa?" I asked.

"This first time I merely toured the colony. When I return again I will make arrangements to meet with several patients."

"When will that be?" I couldn't help wondering, given his vague excuse for putting off a first trip.

"Next month, if I can manage," Goto said.

"One final question." I studied his dark eyes. "Was there anything to suggest to you that Sara's death was not an accident?"

"Not an accident?" Dr. Goto shook his head slowly in apparent disbelief. "How could it be anything else?"

"I'm not sure, doctor. That's why I'm asking you."

"Highly unlikely, unless someone stepped up behind her and . . ."

"Yes, go on."

"But if that were so, how would one account for the mule's broken leg?"

"Good question." I handed him the photo of Parke. "Have you ever seen this man?"

He glanced at the snapshot. "I do not believe so."

"You didn't see him on Moloka'i the day of Sara's death?"

Dr. Goto peered at the photograph again. He turned it so the fluorescent lights would illuminate the snapshot from different angles. Finally he shrugged his sloping shoulders. "No, I did not see him on Moloka'i." He returned the photo.

"Here's my card." I handed it to him. "If you remember anything more about the incident, would you please call me?"

"I will be delighted to help in any way."

I rose and thanked him. "You go much to Las Vegas?" I gestured again to the Caesar's Palace photo on his wall.

"Las Vegas is a fool's paradise," he pontificated. "I avoid it like the plague."

"You'll hang onto more of your money that way." I winked, noting two more clichés.

He smiled his amiable smile as I walked out.

eight

Later that afternoon I called Adrienne to report on the interview with Dr. Goto. I told her that if I had read the doctor right, he honestly didn't know Parke. I was still skeptical, though, about his reasons for taking so long to visit a place so important to his work.

Why would a well-paid physician delay for a dozen years an inexpensive neighbor-island trip? Also suspect was his means of transportation. If Goto were initiating a new research project, wouldn't he have flown to the tiny airstrip that serves Kalaupapa's medical staff, rather than squander time riding a mule like a leisurely tourist?

These things might have nothing to do with the case, but they struck me as odd. Nonetheless, Goto lacked plausible means of murdering Sara and, to all appearances, he lacked a motive as well.

I then called the next two witnesses: Heather Linborg, a masseuse employed by the Wailea Princess Resort on Maui, and Milton Yu, who grew orchids on the Hāmākua Coast of the Big Island. Fortunately, both agreed to see me on short notice.

Unfortunately, the two appointments could be arranged only on the same day, Saturday, and just a few hours apart.

By the time I returned to my apartment, I was ready to surf. My answering machine was blinking, but could wait. I changed quickly into my board shorts.

Surfing relieves the stresses of my detective work and even helps me solve cases. Sherlock Holmes had his pipe—I have my surfboard. Floating on the glassy sea, scanning the blue horizon for the perfect wave, sometimes I drift into a kind of trance. From there I can disentangle the most intricate web.

When my wave finally rolls in, instinct takes over. In one motion I swing the board around, stroke, and rise. Slip-sliding down the thundering cascade, perched on a thin slice of balsa and foam, I find a precarious balance.

That's what surfing and my job are all about: balance.

I grabbed my keys and was heading out the door when my conscience nagged me. *The answering machine.* I stepped back in, one hand still on the handle, and pressed Play.

"Hi there," said the coy, sexy voice. "How's my surfer boy?"

My girlfriend, Niki, calling from California.

"I've got some bad news . . ." She made a little pouting sound. "My flight schedule the next few weeks is murder. Afraid I can't come and see you, baby. I really want to, but I can't. I'm so sorry."

Niki was a Los Angeles-based flight attendant who popped into Honolulu once or twice a month. She was a true California girl: blunt-cut blonde, twenty-seven, and ever ready for fun. Her photo in a string bikini and beaming a heartbreaking smile sits on my nightstand. My cousin Matthew had once called

Niki a "fox"—he meant, I assumed, "good looking," rather than "cunning" and "sly," but he didn't say which.

Niki had requested a home base change, from Los Angeles to Honolulu, so we could spend more time together. Until then, she continued to fly between the West Coast and Denver and Indianapolis. Our relationship was intense but sporadic, like a night of fireworks followed by a month of rain.

I felt sorrier than she did—for myself anyway. I wandered into the kitchen to warm up some Chinese leftovers, and carried them to my *lānai*. On the forty-fifth floor of the Waikīkī Edgewater, you can see for miles. "Edgewater" is a misnomer, since this tower sits nearly a half mile inland from the beach— unless you count the polluted Ala Wai Canal, which the building does indeed border.

My place resembles a Waikīkī hotel room, with kitchen and bath at one end and *lānai* at the other. All that's missing to round out the hotel effect are those tiny complimentary bottles of shampoo, aftershave, and mouthwash. I haven't always lived in Waikīkī. I came here only about a year ago from a cottage in the lush Nu'uanu Valley, just off the Pali Highway. The landlord wouldn't renew my lease—too many broken windows, he had said. And bullet holes in the clapboards. I tried to tell him the damage wasn't my fault, exactly. The friends of a scam artist I had helped to convict decided to get even. Their shots had missed me, but riddled the cottage.

After the landlord booted me I decided to seek the anonymity and round-the-clock security of a Waikīkī condo. Equally compelling were close proximity to O'ahu's most consistent breaks and easy access for Niki. Her airline provided free transportation between the airport and Waikīkī, dropping her a half block from my building. Since Niki's visits were typically brief—less than twenty-four hours—my new location meant more time together. That is, when she was in town, which was becoming less often.

Picking at the lukewarm lemon chicken with my chopsticks, I opened Friday's *Advertiser* to the surf forecast, which promised two-to-four-foot waves on the south shore. That was all the motivation I needed. On my way out the door, I picked up the phone and, against my better judgment, called Niki back.

Her phone rang and rang. Then a sleepy-sounding man with a gruff voice answered, saying that I had the wrong number. I could have sworn I dialed correctly.

I phoned her again. This time I got Niki's answering machine. I told her I missed her and asked when I would see her again.

After hanging up I had a sinking feeling. Niki was indeed a fox—maybe both kinds. I imagined love-hungry corporation men aboard her flights to Denver and Indianapolis, drooling over my California girl.

I didn't often think about what Niki did when we were apart. I didn't let myself. Now I began to wonder.

Within minutes I was paddling my surfboard to my favorite spot in Waikīkī called Populars, a quarter mile offshore of the Sheraton. I navigated the crowded shore break. In Waikīkī, local surfers have to compete for waves with tourists swimming and cavorting on various watercraft. But farther offshore the crowd thins.

I paddled by the crowd toward the long, hollow, fast-breaking rights of Pops. Out here the water is a deep green and the swells come sweeping in. I rode the chest-high waves until it was almost too dark to see, reinvigorating my travel-numbed body and reviving my dampened spirits.

But the surfing brought no new insights into my case. The one revelation of my Moloka'i trip–J. Gregory Parke's appearance at Kalaupapa the day before Sara's death–had yet to be explained. Even if I accepted Adrienne's questionable premise that he had killed Sara, the tougher question still remained: How could he have done it?

When Sara's mule had stumbled, catapulting her down the *pali* to her death, Parke was not among her fellow riders. Could he have enlisted one or more of them to push, trip, or spook the mule in Kaluna's presence? Dr. Goto was an unlikely accomplice, even if his motives for going to Kaluapapa were questionable. The other three witnesses remained to been seen.

nine

Early Saturday morning I flew to Maui. At Kahului Airport I picked up a car and headed south to the sun-splashed resorts of Wailea. Heather Linborg was to meet me at the Wailea Princess at ten o'clock.

Several cases have brought me to Maui before, the most memorable a still-unsolved cane field murder. Actually, it wasn't the investigation that I recalled, but the evening that I wandered into one of Lahaina's jumping oceanfront bars. Two gorgeous flight attendants were sitting at the bar sipping Mai Tais in the sunset, one with a blonde pageboy and quick, wandering eyes.

I don't exactly remember how Niki and I connected. We drank some Mai Tais. Her friend obligingly disappeared. The next thing I knew I woke up staring at the ceiling fan in Niki's hotel room, my body tingling with love's afterglow. She lay naked beside me, dewy and laughing like I had just told a fantastic joke.

"You're *fun!*" She gave me an open-mouthed kiss that seemed to last forever, then breathlessly whispered into my ear: "What was your name?"

That's how we got started—and never looked back. Though that trip to Maui had failed to turn up a cane field murderer, I did uncover one ʻono wahine.

Today, however, there was no time for carousing in the Front Street bars. I hoped my interview with Heather Linborg wouldn't leave as many loose ends as the last one with Dr. Goto had. She said she would be waiting in the Royal Spa, where she worked, near the pool. When I arrived at the immense resort, I realized I should have gotten better directions.

Sprawling over forty acres, the Wailea Princess was one of those magnificent, world-class resorts with every conceivable luxury. A soaring marble foyer, misted by murmuring waterfalls, commanded a breathtaking view of the stunning grounds and white sand beach beyond. The pool was more of a series of pools, meandering through a dazzling tropical landscape with vibrant orchids, anthuriums, proteas, and birds of paradise that put Mrs. Fujiyama's wares to shame. As our appointment neared and the Maui sun blazed overhead, I decided to ask the advice of a groundskeeper who pointed me to the Royal Spa.

I stepped inside the cool marble palace. State-of-the-art saunas, green papaya and tropical enzyme baths, and ocean-view massage rooms dazzled the eye. Patrons roamed the marble aisles in fluffy terry robes. I approached an attendant, a pumped-up bodybuilder who could have stepped off the cover of *Muscle* magazine, and asked for Heather Linborg.

"Heather's sunning." He pointed with an athletic pose to one of the rapids in the swimming pool. His torso glistened. "Look for the gold bikini."

Around the pool I saw several women in bikinis sunning, but only one glinted like a newly minted coin. It was a brilliant, mirror-like suit designed for show, rather than for swimming.

This woman had plenty to show: the breasts of a porn star, barely contained by her string bikini, and long, silky-looking legs.

"Heather Linborg?" I asked hopefully.

She put down her paperback book, *The Bridges of Madison County.*

"This is such a good book. I've been crying all the way through," she said in a shrill little voice that set me on edge. I noticed a small birthmark on her face resembling a dark heart— the only visible flaw to her otherwise calendar-girl looks.

I handed her my card. She glanced at it and raised her two perfectly penciled eyebrows. "You're a *surfing* detective?"

I nodded and sat on the edge of the lounge chair next to hers. "I just have some routine questions. Your recollections about the accident could be helpful."

"It was awful," Heather replied, instantly transported to that day. "I wish I'd never taken that mule ride."

"Do you mind my asking why you visited Kalaupapa?"

"I wanted to see the leper colony before it gets overrun by tourists." Heather crossed her tanned-to-perfection legs.

"And you're afraid it will be overrun soon?"

"Isn't that what's happening on all the islands?"

"This place isn't exactly the outback." I gestured to the Royal Spa, which was crawling with terry-clad patrons.

"I also do freelance jobs," she said, then frowned, as if she'd revealed a trade secret.

"About the accident, could you describe to me what happened?"

"I'm probably not the best one to ask. I rode up front near the guide. Sara was behind me. I didn't see her fall."

"What did you see?"

"Well, she screamed, so I turned. I saw the mule collapsed on the trail. One of its legs was apparently broken."

"Kaluna, the guide, was pretty shook up about that mule," I said. "Coco was his favorite."

"You know, the mule didn't seem to suffer. It just lay there with a calm look in its eyes."

"Had you met Sara before the mule tour?"

"I'd heard of her, of course. But I'd never met her before."

"What was your opinion of her?"

"I liked her. She was real and personable and very bright."

I pulled out the photo of Parke. "Have you ever seen this man?"

Heather winced. Then she composed herself. "No, I've never seen him." I noticed a drip of perspiration trickling down her forehead.

"Never? Not at Kalaupapa? Not anywhere?"

"No . . ." She wiped her brow. "I never saw him at Kalaupapa or anywhere else."

I tried to mask my disbelief with a faint smile. *Check for connections between Parke and Linborg,* I entered into my mental notebook.

She abruptly handed me the photo. "Got to run. Massage appointment in five minutes."

Heather rose, clutching *The Bridges of Madison County.* I watched the dancing glint of her gold bikini in the Maui sun as she walked away.

ten

Why had Heather Linborg lied? She obviously knew Parke. But in what capacity, I wanted to know.

People are like waves, I thought as my Hilo-bound plane rumbled over Kahului Bay. On the surface they may sparkle and gleam, but what really matters lies below. The most glassy tube can be the most dangerous. Under its luminous green barrel may hide a jagged reef—one heartbeat beneath the rushing foam.

Whether surfing or working a case, I've learned to keep my eyes open. Otherwise, I'd be a dead surfer by now. And a dead detective.

Below the climbing jet, the fabled Hāna Highway twisted and curved along the coastline. Inland, emerald canyons of bamboo, breadfruit, and flowering 'ōhi'ā were pierced by silver waterfalls. As we glided over this craggy coast with majestic Haleakalā towering in the distance, I wondered if Heather had served Parke as a masseuse. And had she given him a mere rubdown? Or something more personal? That she knew him at all seemed ominous.

Soon the Big Island came into view. As the jet descended down the Hāmākua Coast, I saw lime green *kukui* and the fire orange flowers of African tulip dotting the landscape in brilliant contrast. Above these flamboyant trees rose Mauna Kea, Hawai'i's tallest mountain, cloud shrouded and dominating.

By one o'clock I had picked up my second rental car of the day and was driving north on Bayfront Highway. Milton Yu, the orchid grower, lived thirty miles north of Hilo, *mauka* of the old plantation town of Pa'auilo. I would make our two o'clock appointment in good time.

My hasty background check on Yu had turned up his former occupation as a computer consultant, and his arrest for possession of marijuana. Apparently, the quantity of *pakalōlō* had been small or the evidence circumstantial, because the case was promptly dropped and just as promptly Yu left O'ahu for the Big Island. He was either very lucky or very well connected.

Pa'auilo turned out to be a sleepy village whose decaying sugar mill, like others on this depressed coast, stood abandoned. Following Yu's directions, I turned onto a narrow paved road, climbing past rotting plantation houses and a small farm or two. As the road rose higher through fallow cane fields, the air cooled and brought fog. In a few miles, the pavement ended and the path turned red. My car kept climbing.

Beneath mist-shrouded Mauna Kea, on a plateau surrounded by jungle, sat Yu's redwood cottage. The soaring A-frame and encircling *lānai* suggested money—on a clear day, it would command an incredible view of the Hāmākua Coast. Behind the cottage stood a huge greenhouse. And beyond that, acres of jungle and rain forest.

As I pulled into the gravel drive, a local Chinese man in faded jeans, a Grateful Dead sweatshirt, and rubber slippers emerged from the cottage. He was slim and looked to be in his early forties. His raven hair, prematurely grey, hung in a ponytail.

"Milton?" I stepped from my car into the cool mountain air and shook his hand.

Up close, Yu's shy, dark eyes had a deer-in-the-headlights look and were riddled with tiny red veins. I noticed his sweatshirt smelled faintly of smoke—though not tobacco and not wood.

Yu motioned me to follow him to his *lānai*, which was lined with a variety of colorful orchids—lavender, cream, yellow, deep purple. We sat in his two rattan chairs. The vista took in miles of sloping fields blanketed by fog. After some preliminaries in pidgin about his retirement from the computer business, I turned our discussion to the case.

"Milton, why you like go to Kalaupapa?"

"Da rare plants," Yu replied in a voice as shy as his eyes. "Kalaupapa get some you nevah see on da Big Island."

"Fo' real? You wen' find rare kine dere?"

"Some." Yu averted his eyes. "But on da tour dere's nevah time fo' collecting, yeah?" He glanced at his watch.

"On da ride up da *pali*, you wen' see Sara fall?"

"No, was behind me. Heard one loud scream, brah—*really* loud—den rustle in da bushes down below . . ." He paused. "Den nut'ing. The *haole* guy wen' ride behind her saw da whole t'ing."

"Archibald, da travel agent?"

"From da mainland, I t'ink."

"What Archibald do aftah da accident?"

"He stare ovah da cliff. He nevah do nut'ing. Jus' stare."

"You t'ink he involved?"

"In da accident?" Yu's eyes suddenly looked confused.

"Maybe he wen' push her or somet'ing li' dat?"

"Why ask me? I no can see nut'ing."

"But you wen' talk wit' her during da ride, eh?"

"Yeah, we wen' talk. Shoots, she one foxy babe—an' *akamai*."

"*Akamai* how?"

"Smart, you know. Like one professor or somet'ing. She say she give one lecture, brah, dat night."

"Lecture? She say where?"

"In Kaunakakai. At one health food store."

"I hearing dis right? She say she goin' talk at one health food store?"

He nodded and looked again at his watch.

"What she wen' talk about?"

"I dunno." He shrugged, warping the smile of the late, grey-bearded Grateful Dead bandleader. "Maybe she one vegetarian or somet'ing."

I pulled out the photo of J. Gregory Parke. "Evah see dis guy?"

Yu glanced at the photo and nodded. "Used to come into da computah store. He rich. He buy computahs like dey bin toys."

"You see dis guy Parke at Kalaupapa when Sara fall?"

"Nah." Yu rose abruptly.

"Thanks, eh?" Before he disappeared, I added, "Befo' I go, you like show me da kine rare orchid?"

A cloud crossed Yu's face, making him appear reluctant rather than proud to display his gems. He led me slowly into the redwood cottage. The rancid, musty odor of *pakalōlō*—literally "numbing tobacco"—filled the main room. Only about a half dozen orchids stood near his *makai* windows.

Yu ambled from one rare flower to another, softly uttering their Latin names. He then mumbled something about his business and pointed to an elaborate office with numerous electronic gadgets—a fax, photocopier, two computers, several phones with caller ID units, a cb radio, and a police scanner that crackled with distant voices. It seemed like far more equipment than a former computer consultant needed and certainly more than that of a fledgling orchid grower.

I handed Yu my card and asked him to call me collect if he remembered anything else about Sara's death, though I doubted he would. His phone rang. He answered it as I found my own way out, snooping as discreetly as I could.

Parked behind the cottage was a new Range Rover—black on black—a luxury four-wheel-drive dream wagon for the outback. I peeked inside at the leather seats, cell phone, scanner, and radar detector. Pretty high-tech for an orchid guru.

By three I was driving back toward Hilo. Milton Yu had given me something new to go on: Sara's lecture at the health food store in Kaunakakai. My background check on her had turned up no prior speeches or articles about either health food or vegetarianism. What would have been her subject?

I believed Yu was telling the truth about Sara, but not about his own occupation. His possible connection to the islands' drug underworld would require some further investigation.

Back in Hilo I made a call to the health food store, but the manager there told me that Sara had only alluded to the topic of her speech as "a matter of concern to all Moloka'i residents." Her reputation, if not celebrity, must have been enough to draw a crowd.

I then checked into Uncle Willy's Hilo Bay, and drank a beer in front of the evening news. The lead story was about a Honolulu man who had disappeared while fishing from a rock ledge at Bamboo Ridge, near the Hālona Blowhole on the southeastern tip of Oʻahu. The twenty-three-year-old law student, Baron Taniguchi, still hadn't been found. Sipping my beer, I wondered if Taniguchi had ever taken a course from Sara Ridgely-Parke.

eleven

At sunset on Sunday evening I met Adrienne for drinks at the Halekūlani. More than a few rungs above Uncle Willy's, my client's hotel was the ritziest on Waikīkī Beach. I was surprised she had agreed to cocktails at this violet hour, but she sounded anxious to hear the details of my recent interviews. We had planned to meet early, since the next morning I would fly to Los Angeles to interview the last witness, Emery Archibald. Only he had been in a position to observe Sara's fall. Would Archibald shed light on what was beginning to seem a very suspicious accident?

Adrienne arrived wearing a baby blue dress that deepened the color of her eyes. I followed her subtly alluring scent to a table under the spreading boughs of the century-old *kiawe* tree that reigns over the Halekūlani's outdoor *lānai*. Named "House Without a Key," after the Charlie Chan mystery, this seemed an appropriate place to discuss our potential murder case. As the cocktail waitress brought us Maui chips and took our order, I noticed the sweet sound of a slack-key guitar tune coming from the *lānai's* small stage, backlighted by red-gold arcs of the setting sun.

"So tell me," Adrienne said while we waited for our drinks, "do you have enough evidence to indict Greg Parke for the murder?"

"We have a ways to go before we can indict anybody, Adrienne. Parke included."

"I told you, no one would want to kill my sister more than her ex-husband."

"We'll see. I have an interview Tuesday in L.A. with the travel agent who rode behind Sara when she fell. If anyone can provide us more clues, it'll be him."

"How many witnesses besides the mule guide recognized Greg's photo?"

"Two. One admitted knowing him, the other didn't."

"One lied?"

I nodded. "The one who admitted knowing Parke is Milton Yu. He used to sell computers in Honolulu. Now he grows orchids on the Big Island, but that's just a cover for *pakalōlō*. Yu may be deep into the drug trade, or just a small supplier."

"What could he have to do with Sara's death?"

"Maybe nothing. Maybe everything."

"And the witness who lied?"

"Heather Linborg, a Maui masseuse. She winced when she saw Parke's photo. It would be interesting to find out why."

The waitress appeared with two Chi Chis, tall goblets frothing like milkshakes. They even tasted like milkshakes, with a coconut and pineapple sweetness that masked double shots of vodka. I raised my glass to Adrienne, stifling the impulse to make a toast, since this was hardly a date. Our glasses clinked.

"Let's look at what we have so far." I took a swallow of the icy drink and set my glass down. "If Parke had your sister murdered, who would he have hired to do it? And how would he have gotten the mule to cooperate?"

"What about the mule guide?"

"Kaluna's a *paniolo*. I don't think he'd harm a mule to kill anybody."

"And the doctor?"

"Dr. Goto didn't look like the type to handle mules. He told me he'd always wanted to do medical research at Kalaupapa, yet put off his first visit a dozen years. That makes me wonder. Though I doubt he conspired with Parke."

"Why not?" Adrienne sipped her Chi Chi.

"Goto doesn't know Parke. I could tell by his response to the photo."

"That leaves the Californian. Archibald has got to be the one."

"We can't write off the others just yet. Yu and Linborg both know Parke, and both are hiding something. Which reminds me, Yu said Sara planned to give a lecture at a health food store in Kaunakakai that same night. Any idea what that would have been about?"

"Sara gave public lectures all the time," Adrienne replied coolly. "She didn't bother to tell me the subject of each one." Adrienne turned her chilly gaze to the dying sunset, as if she was searching for something.

That was an unexpected response to what I thought was an innocuous question. I watched Adrienne's frozen expression, but it didn't change. I swallowed the last of my Chi Chi and ordered two more when the waitress passed by. Then I remembered a burning question I had neglected to ask Adrienne on our first meeting.

"When did you last speak with Sara?"

Adrienne kept looking into the twilight, as she sipped the last of her drink. "I can't recall."

"A few days? A month?"

She gazed down into her empty glass, then spoke in an uncharacteristically quiet voice. "Five years."

"Five years?" I stared at her. "You told me you and your sister were 'very close.'"

"We *were* close. But Sara was strong willed and so am I. Before she moved to Hawai'i we had a disagreement."

"So you never came to the islands to see her?"

"No."

"She never came to Boston to see you?"

Adrienne shook her head.

"And you never wrote or talked on the phone?"

"No."

This wasn't making any sense. "But you inherited her entire estate—four million dollars?"

Adrienne glanced up at the approaching cocktail waitress and smiled wryly, as if relieved for the interruption. The waitress gathered our spent drinks, set down fresh napkins, then placed frothing new goblets on them.

Adrienne waited for the waitress to leave. "Things happen between sisters that a man wouldn't understand."

She looked out again toward the darkening ocean, her lips set in a tight line. I decided not to press her further on what seemed to be a sensitive issue. The time would come.

As we reached the bottom of our second drinks, the moon was rising over Diamond Head. The singer crooned "Blue Hawai'i," his voice as gentle as the soothing tropical breeze: *"Come with me when the moon is on the sea . . ."*

Despite my objections, Adrienne put the Chi Chis on her hotel tab. When we stood I felt a bit wobbly. I wondered where her idea of the evening ended.

"Walk on the beach?" I suggested. "The moonlight is magic on the water."

She looked hesitant a first, then seemed to make an instant decision. "That'd be perfect."

I let her lead us to the shore, where she took her heels off and stepped onto the sand. A few off-balance strides put us at the ocean's edge. I steadied her by putting my hands around her slender waist.

Being that close to her, touching her, breathing in her perfumed scent made me almost dizzy. I wanted this woman. I had from the start. She looked at me with those eyes that kept turning from steel grey to baby blue.

By the time we returned to the Halekūlani we were strolling arm in arm like lovers. In the elevator she pressed "12," the doors closed, and we kissed. Before the doors opened again, we had abandoned ourselves to our Chi Chi-inflamed passions.

Down the hall, Adrienne hung a Do Not Disturb sign on the door of her oceanfront suite. I opened the *lānai* doors and let in the moonlight. She slipped off her dress and lay on the bed in the moon's buttery glow. As I unbuttoned my aloha shirt, Adrienne's eyes opened wide. The welts on my chest. I started to explain–but she stopped me. With a whisper-soft touch she drew me down on her.

twelve

Before leaving Adrienne's suite by the waning moonlight, my head still spinning, I had somehow managed to ask her to phone the University of Hawai'i Law School about Baron Taniguchi, the missing fisherman. Could he have been one of Sara's former students? Adrienne had agreed to call while I was in Los Angeles.

Five hours later, I was dragging myself aboard a crowded DC-10. Booking a last-minute fare had landed me in the cramped middle section of the coach cabin. I desperately needed sleep, but every time I tried to snooze, another passenger crawled over me to stretch or use the lavatory. Every time, I awoke with an aching head.

The airliner touched down in Los Angeles just as the setting sun tinted the hazy gray sky. I couldn't help thinking of Niki as we taxied to the terminal. I decided to call her that night from my hotel.

In the darkening twilight I picked up a car and crawled through Monday rush-hour traffic toward the suburb of Glendale. I checked in at the Red Lion Hotel, about a half mile from Archibald's travel agency, Island Fantasy Holidays. Archibald had agreed to see me the next morning at nine. Still spent from my late night and long flight, I ordered dinner in my room. Then I slipped between the crisp king-sized sheets, all too reminiscent of Adrienne's moonlit bed at the Halekūlani.

I reached for the nightstand phone and started to dial Niki's number. I put the receiver back in its holder. Why not just drop by tomorrow on my way back to the airport? Maybe I'd discover the truth about what she'd been doing when we were apart. Hopefully she wouldn't have flown off to Denver or Indianapolis.

I fell asleep, reminiscing of those first few nights Niki and I spent together.

Tuesday morning I pulled up to Island Fantasy Holidays, which, according to a mauve marquee, specialized in Hawai'i vacations. The agency occupied one of several units in an upscale strip mall along Glenoaks Boulevard. The outer office smelled of new carpet and paint, which were both in soft pastels and illuminated by indirect lighting. New Age music wafted through speakers in the ceiling. The agency looked prosperous.

A twenty-something blonde, reminding me too much of Niki, directed me to an inner office, its wall lined with brass plaques. As I entered, a slim, elegant man in pinstripes rose behind his desk. His maroon ascot and tortoiseshell glasses gave him a dapper, almost flamboyant look. His full head of wavy copper hair had greyed handsomely at the temples. He was probably pushing fifty, but looked younger. Reaching for his offered hand, I whiffed the spicy aroma of his aftershave.

"Mr. Archibald, thank you for seeing me."

"Call me Emery." He winked. "Emery Archibald, the third. Grandfather started this travel business a half century ago. I'm his namesake."

"You've kept the business in your family a long time. You must be proud."

"We are." With an aristocratic flourish of fingers, Archibald straightened his tortoiseshell glasses. His gold wedding band gleamed. "I hope you didn't fly all the way from Honolulu just for this interview."

"Don't worry," I reassured him. "I have other business in Los Angeles."

"I'm relieved, since I can't tell you anything about the accident that I didn't already tell the police."

"Then I hope you don't mind going over the same territory again, for my client's peace of mind."

"Not at all." Archibald ran his fingers through his copper hair.

"May I ask you first why you were on Moloka'i the day of the accident?"

"Certainly." Archibald again straightened his glasses. "Let me give you some background. A few years ago, I changed the name of our agency from 'Archibald's' to 'Island Fantasy Holidays.' The original name sounded a bit old fashioned; besides, Hawaiian vacations had become our bread and butter."

"From those awards on your wall, it appears you've been very successful." I gestured to the armada of plaques from the Hawai'i Tourism Board, United Airlines, Hertz, Hilton, Sheraton, and a dozen others. Next to those hung a photo of him with a cozy group whom I guessed to be his wife and children.

"Hawai'i has been good to us, though the future looks cloudy."

"Why's that?"

"The airlines have cut our commissions." Archibald began toying with a maroon fountain pen. "It's tough. Very tough. Some smaller agencies have already gone under."

"But you're hanging on?"

"We book vacation packages—hotels, rental cars, tours— whole trips in tickets and coupons. That's what saves us. That's what took me to Moloka'i."

"I don't quite understand."

"To keep abreast of island tours available to our clients, I actually take them myself. I can sell a tour better if I've been on it first . . ." He leaned back in his leather chair. "Moloka'i is on the verge of a tourism boom. What's happening on Lāni'i is nothing compared to what you'll see soon on Moloka'i. More hotels, more resorts, more daily flights."

"Why do you believe tourism will boom?"

"Simple. Once Kalaupapa becomes a fully operational National Park and that new Chancellor Trust resort goes in on the cliffs above it, the sky's the limit."

"So you took the tour in hopes of developing new business for your agency?"

"Precisely."

"Did you go alone, or did your family join you?" I nodded toward the portrait on his wall.

"The two boys had a swim meet here." Archibald again preened his copper hair. "Martha stayed home with them and our daughter. I went alone."

"About the accident . . ."

"Terrible. She was a lovely woman."

"You knew Sara Ridgely-Parke?"

"Oh, no—that is, not before this trip. We just got to chatting and she had these marvelous ideas about 'ecotourism'—you know, packages that stimulate nature lovers to travel, which of course would boost our business."

"Ecotourism was apparently a favorite theme of hers."

"She seemed to be a brilliant woman. Brilliant. That makes her passing all the more tragic."

"During the mule ride when Sara fell, where were you riding in relation to her?"

"I rode behind her by about ten feet. The mule stumbled, I heard her scream, and the poor woman hurtled over the cliff."

"Just like that?"

"Everyone was shocked. There seemed no reason for it to happen. Least of all to her, the only one of us who had experience riding, except of course for the guide."

"Before the mule collapsed, did it do anything out of the ordinary?"

"Well, let me think." Archibald rocked back in his chair. "It passed some gas."

"Farted?"

Archibald cracked a smile.

"Ah, did anyone feed it anything or behave suspiciously around it?"

Archibald shook his head. "We were with the animals all the time, except during the bus tour of Kalaupapa. Then the mules were tethered together under some trees."

"Did all five riders take the bus tour?"

He nodded. "Only the skinner stayed behind with his animals."

I pulled out the photo of Parke and set it on his desk. "Recognize this man?"

Archibald puzzled over the image. "Should I recognize him?"

"Not necessarily."

"I'm drawing a blank." He returned it, his expression suggesting he was telling the truth.

As I put the photo away, a muscular adolescent ambled in wearing a canary yellow tank top that said, "Gold's Gym." His biceps bulged, as if he had just pumped them up. On one muscular arm a bloody dagger was tattooed. *A rebellious son?*

"Stephan here is my assistant." Archibald handed his boyish helper some airline tickets. The two exchanged glances. A current of energy seemed to flow between them. I couldn't imagine what it might mean.

After Stephan departed I gave Archibald my card and asked him to call if he remembered anything more about the accident. Except for his fussy appearance and odd interchange with the boy, I found little reason to suspect the travel agent of anything. Nor had he provided me with much new information.

Had I flown all the way to Los Angeles to learn only that the victim's mount had passed gas? A five-hour flight for a mule fart?

By ten that morning I had checked out of the Red Lion and was heading back toward the L.A. airport. My flight to Honolulu didn't depart until two, so I had plenty of time to visit Niki.

A few mile's drive north of the airport on Pacific Coast Highway brought Marina Del Rey, a pleasure-boat harbor where sun-loving pilots and flight attendants reside. Niki lived in a condo called La Casa Nova, a pink stucco complex surrounded by a wrought iron fence. Since I wanted to surprise her, I didn't use the intercom to clear the security gate, but waited for someone to come along with a key.

The lushly landscaped Casa Nova consisted of several wings built around a heart-shaped swimming pool. Niki's apartment was 309-F. I hoofed up to the third floor of the F wing, then flew past a dozen apartments. My breathing was fast by the time I reached 309.

I knocked and listened with growing anticipation as I heard oddly heavy, lumbering footsteps inside. My smile tightened on my face as the door swung open.

My smile fell.

Standing before me was not Niki, but a middle-aged airline pilot who looked as if he had just crash-landed. His pilot's uniform was wrinkled, his ruddy face shadowed by mostly grey whiskers, and his eyes bloodshot.

"Who are you?" I asked.

"Captain Jacoby," he said in a gravelly voice. "Who the hell are *you?*"

I glanced inside the dark and disordered apartment, feeling suddenly short of breath. "Where's Niki?"

"Flying to Denver." He looked me up and down. "Why do you want to know?"

"Niki is . . ." I hesitated. "She's an old friend."

The pilot folded his arms across his chest. He seemed annoyed at having to deal with me at all during his catnap. I imagined it was his voice that greeted me when I had called Niki's number from Hawai'i. I wondered what stories she'd been making up to tell him.

"I was in the area and thought I'd see if Niki . . . still lived here." Then I added in a more conciliatory tone, "Have you two been together long?"

"A year or so." His face was registering suspicion. "So who should I say stopped by?"

A year? I could tell I'd lost this battle before it had even started. "Oh, it's been so long, she probably wouldn't even remember me."

I turned to leave and could feel the pilot's eyes on my back as I walked dejectedly down the hall.

thirteen

On my long flight back across the Pacific, I knew I shouldn't feel sorry for myself. I had no one to blame for Niki's fooling me but my own blind eye. I'd told her I didn't want to know what she did when I wasn't around. I guess she'd taken my request seriously.

Later in my studio, I mechanically went through my evening ritual of reading Honolulu's two daily papers. A back-page story in the *Star-Bulletin* caught my eye: "Missing Fisherman's Tackle Found."

In the trunk of an abandoned unregistered car near Makapu'u Point—miles from where law student Baron Taniguchi disappeared—his tackle had been recovered. Investigators originally attributed the accident to heavy surf. But now that his tackle had turned up, foul play was a possibility.

The article said Taniguchi was an experienced fisherman who had fished the rugged coastline since boyhood. Number two in his class, he had been serving as an intern for the Good Government Hotline, a sounding board for public service complaints and a hotline for confidential tips on suspected government corruption. The Hotline had been established by a small group of reformed-minded state legislators after a *New York Times* article exposed a too cozy relationship between some island politicians and land developers.

I called Adrienne immediately. She wasn't in. I left a message on the Halekūlani's voice mail: "I'll be in my office by one tomorrow. Come by if you can and bring anything you've found on Baron Taniguchi."

The next morning I drove around the windward side of the island to Waimānalo, a proud Hawaiian town of humble plantation cottages and oceanfront estates. It was the closest civilization to Makapuʻu Point, where Taniguchi's tackle had been found.

"Nalo-town," as locals call it, has a bizarre attraction—among its rustic dwellings is an evergreen-ringed polo field, complete with grandstands and a white picket fence suitable for an English lord. The incongruity between these two worlds has always struck me as odd. But contrasts of old and new, kamaʻāina and foreign immigrants are commonplace in the islands.

The politics of the polo field, however, was not what brought me today to Waimānalo. Where there is polo, there are ponies. And where there are ponies, there are large-animal veterinarians.

I tracked down Dr. Otto Frenz, who, according to the State Animal Quarantine Station, was the island's foremost authority on horses and mules. I met with Dr. Frenz in the paddock of a horse stable just outside of town. The native of Austria was robust and ruddy cheeked, with a barrel chest and frosty blue Santa Claus eyes.

I described the accident on Moloka'i, which the doctor recalled, and asked him how it might have happened.

"Das mule ist much like das horse." He spoke with a thick German accent. "Ven he ist spooked or, how do you say . . . ill, he vill stumble."

"This mule was neither, according to the guide and four witnesses."

"*Ach!* No symptoms?"

"None." I thought for a moment. "Though one witness said it passed gas."

"Hmmm . . ." The doctor scratched his chin. "Ven did das mule last eat?"

"In Kalaupapa village before the ascent, I think."

"Maybe digestion?" Dr. Frenz asked, as if talking to himself.

"Could that be all?"

"Vat about drugs? Das mule vas medicated?"

"Not according to the guide."

"Hmmm." The doctor again stroked his chin. "Very interesting. I vill check das veterinary journal and vill call you."

I thanked Dr. Frenz and handed him my card.

"Der 'Surfing Detective'!" He squinted at the card, then launched into a lengthy story about once meeting Tom Selleck when he was shooting a horseback-riding scene for an episode of *Magnum P.I.* The animated story went on and on.

"Der *Magnum* ist goot guy," the doctor concluded. I replied that many people had told me the same and then slipped away.

Driving back toward town, I turned off at the Hālona Blowhole and parked among tourists watching the natural sea spout shoot like Old Faithful into the air. About a hundred yards to the west of the Blowhole lay Bamboo Ridge, a narrow slab of hardened lava perched over heaving seas where fisherman traditionally cast their bamboo poles. Baron Taniguchi had hiked to this treacherous ledge the day of his disappearance. A novice angler could easily be swept away here, but Taniguchi was no novice. He knew this coastline. And from what I knew about cliff fishing, you don't leave your tackle at the top—the climb back up for more hooks or sinkers or leaders is too steep.

Taniguchi's gear had been found at Makapu'u Point, two miles away, which didn't make sense. Driving back to town along these surf-battered cliffs, I considered what possible connection might have existed between Taniguchi and Sara Ridgely-Parke.

Waiting to meet Adrienne in my office that afternoon, I wondered how our one night together would affect our working relationship. Adrienne arrived and from the way she swept her eyes nonchalantly over my ramshackle office, I saw she wanted to pretend nothing had happened. She was avoiding looking at me directly, and the few times she did, all I saw on her face was a cool, New England reserve. Apparently she had drawn a crisp line between business and pleasure.

"Did you see this morning's paper?" she asked, pulling out a copy of today's *Advertiser*.

I hadn't.

"*Pakalōlō* King Held Without Bail." Under this headline was a photo of ponytailed Milton Yu in handcuffs, still wearing his musty Grateful Dead sweatshirt. Yu had been charged with masterminding a multimillion dollar underground trade in cannabis.

While Yu's arrest for drug trafficking didn't necessarily make him a more likely murder suspect, his connection to organized crime got me thinking. Could Sara's activism in

Hawai'i have threatened this Big Island *pakalōlō* grower or his comrades? Seemed like another long shot. This case was spawning them like cane spiders.

Then a dark cloud crossed my mind. If Milton Yu believed I had turned him in, there would soon be—if not already—a price on my head. Some "mokes," big, local thugs, might be gunning for me right now. Not a pretty thought. It gave me chicken skin.

"Yu admitted to knowing Greg," Adrienne said. "There's got to be some link to Sara's death. Maybe Greg's mixed up in drug dealing. Maybe that's where some of his money comes from."

"Doubtful. Why would a developer like J. Gregory Parke, who's made millions in construction, dabble in a risky venture like trafficking dope?"

"Still, he could be involved with Yu."

"I'll see what I can find out from Parke himself when I interview him tomorrow."

Adrienne tensed.

"By the way," I said, wondering at her sudden edginess, "what did you learn at the U.H. Law School about Baron Taniguchi? Did he take any classes from Sara?"

"The school refused to tell me anything." She relaxed back in her seat. "We can order his transcript, but only with his permission."

"Catch-22."

"And what if Taniguchi did take classes from my sister? What's the point?"

"It's just a hunch. Sometimes a hunch leads nowhere. Sometimes it cracks a case wide open."

Our eyes met and I noticed a hint of baby blue in the slate hue of Adrienne's gaze. I made a bold move.

"How about dinner tonight? We can even eat this time."

A faint smile showed through her composure.

"Tonight I'm meeting one of Sara's law school colleagues, Rush McWhorter."

"McWhorter? Wasn't he your sister's adversary, and counsel for the Chancellor Trust?"

"Actually, Rush respected Sara. He knew her quite well. That's why I'm having dinner with him—to see if he can give us any more clues."

"Well, let me know how it goes."

"I'm sure it will go fine." Adrienne rose. "By the way, when you see Greg Parke tomorrow, don't take seriously anything he says about me."

She turned and strode coolly from my office, leaving me wondering about her parting words. *What could Parke possibly have on Adrienne?*

fourteen

On the brief jaunt from my apartment to Parke's Kāhala estate the next day, I passed some of the most expensive real estate in America. Kāhala Avenue stretches for over a mile between Diamond Head and the Wai'alae Country Club, and is graced by waterfront estates, each with its guest houses, servants' quarters, pool and spa, tennis courts, and secluded beach. Few properties in Kāhala, even on the back streets, sell below one million.

In Sara's campaign for affordable housing, she had argued that the continued climb in property values would soon reduce the islands' population to two classes—the rich and those who clean their toilets. Yet, ironically, during her marriage to Parke, Sara herself had called this ritzy neighborhood home.

Parke had made his millions erecting high-rise condominiums and office towers. He had poured his profits into Hawai'i real estate before Japanese investment more than doubled values in the mid-eighties, then he sat back and watched his fortune multiply. I still found it odd that Sara, noted environmentalist and champion of affordable housing, should marry a man so opposed to her causes. Another case of *Sleeping with the Enemy?* What could attract two people so apparently unlike?

Parke's oceanfront estate couldn't be seen from the street. His mansion lay behind copper gates etched with dolphins frolicking in cobalt blue surf, deep within a forest of Manila palms. I announced myself on the intercom, and one of the handsome gates opened automatically. In front of the white-columned pseudo-colonial home was a cream Rolls Royce convertible whose plate said, "JGP 3." *If a Rolls is his third car, what does Parke drive as cars one and two?*

Beyond the mansion's fluted columns, *koa* double doors graced with more cavorting dolphins slowly opened. A short, bald, pink-skinned man waved me in. Soon I discovered this was not a servant, but Parke himself. He was round as a meatball in wrinkled Bermudas and a golf shirt that was stretched over his humpty-dumpty gut and stained with something bright orange like taco sauce. He stood only about five feet in his bare feet, and from the leather-like creases in his pink face and the grey sideburns beneath his shiny dome, he appeared to be easily twenty years older than his deceased ex-wife.

Parke led me through an enormous living room, carpeted in plush Berber wool, and bigger than my flat and office combined. Then we stepped down into a sunken bar that opened onto a steaming spa and, beyond that, the blue Pacific.

"What can I get you to drink?" Parke stepped behind the rose-hued granite bar, his pink scalp reflecting the afternoon sun through a skylight.

"Make it club soda," I said. "My clients unfortunately don't pay me to drink on the job."

"I'll have the same. With a splash of Scotch." Parke eyed the Scotch bottle furtively, as if it were his secret lover.

He loaded two crystal cocktail glasses with ice cubes, then poured fizzing club soda to the brim in mine, and half full in his. He filled remainder of his glass with Chivas Regal. I watched as the aromatic gold Scotch turned a shade paler in the bubbling water. I took my plain club soda from him and we toasted.

Despite Parke's sloppy appearance, he had shrewd, intelligent eyes and a magnetism I found strangely attractive. Rich, self-made men often strike me this way. But beneath his aura, I detected one of those hidden things I'm prone to discover in people and waves. I just couldn't fathom what.

After we exchanged a few pleasantries, Parke clinked his Scotch glass on the granite bar. "Now what can I tell you about my former wife?"

I decided to jump right in. "It puzzles me, Mr. Parke, that two people so different should marry." I watched his expression for change. "I mean, Sara being anti-development and you a developer."

"We weren't as different as you might think," he replied without a pause or blink. "Although we first met as adversaries at a hearing on Coconut Beach. I spoke on behalf of a friend of mine who proposed to develop a parcel across from the beach. Sara represented the Save Coconut Beach coalition, who opposed my friend."

"And Sara won?"

"Of course she won. And it's a damn good thing, because Sara wasn't a good loser." He made a grunting sound that was either a tight laugh or a groan. "Don't let those glowing sentiments you read about her fool you. Sara was tough. She could get down and dirty."

"Did you admire her for that?" I sipped my club soda.

"As I said, we were more alike than you might imagine. We both played to win." Parke eyed his Scotch, its color lightening as the ice cubes melted. "I found that out the hard way in divorce court. Sara tried to take my home. *This* home." He gestured to the sunken bar and mammoth living room, then outside to the sun-splashed spa. "She didn't invest a dime in it—not one damn dime—and she tried to take it all. Square that with her liberal causes!" He gulped half his Chivas in a swallow.

"How did the court settle it?"

"The judge was a woman and she was crooked." Parke wiped his Scotch-glazed lips with his hand. "Sara had no legitimate claim to any of my assets, yet that damn judge awarded her half of my home."

"That must have added up to a sizable piece of change."

"Then what does Sara do with the money? She buys a half acre of oceanfront at Lanikai, all the while claiming to be a champion of affordable housing!"

"Sounds like a contradiction." I tried to keep him going.

"Sara was full of contradictions." Parke poured more Scotch into his half-empty glass, again giving it a golden glow. "Publicly she criticized developers like me. Privately she adored our perks and privileges."

"That's not just sour grapes, is it?"

"Sour grapes!" Parke's face turned a brighter pink. "I listened in court to all those lies about me while keeping my mouth shut to save Sara's reputation."

"From what?"

"Sara cheated."

"She was unfaithful?"

"There were many men." Parke raised both fleshy hands in a gesture of philosophical resignation. "But I'll tell you only one: McWhorter."

"Rush McWhorter? Her colleague at the law school?"

Parke nodded and sipped his Scotch, his anger seeming to have passed. I made a mental note to talk with Rush McWhorter sooner rather than later, then shifted gears.

"Mr. Parke, why did you travel to Moloka'i the day before your ex-wife's death?"

Parke slammed down his glass on the bar, nearly shattering it. "How did you know?"

"You were identified by several people."

Parke looked into his Chivas, then peered at me with watery, searching eyes. "Sara was bad to me in court, but I just couldn't get over her."

Suddenly I realized the "hidden thing" I had detected in Parke: The wealthy developer was a painfully lonely man. He pined for his ex-wife.

"I wanted to see Sara." Parke cleared his throat. "I had called her a few days before to invite her to dinner. She declined, saying she was going on the Moloka'i mule ride the next day. So I flew over there. But she didn't show—she had given me the wrong date. Maybe on purpose. Maybe by mistake." Parked looked dejected as if it had all just happened to him.

"Does the name Milton Yu sound familiar?" I shifted gears quickly again, not wanting him to lose momentum.

"Too bad about Yu. He should have stuck with computers. *Pakalōlō* did him in."

"And Heather Linborg? She's a Maui masseuse who seems to know you."

"Yes, I've met Heather, but she could have nothing to do with Sara's death. And by the way, is Sara's sister paying you to dredge up this garbage?"

"Sorry, I can't say."

"You don't need to. If anyone was capable of harming Sara it was Adrienne. She stole Sara's fiancé back in Boston and Sara never forgave her."

"Then why did Sara leave her everything?"

"Adrienne was Sara's only family. But after we divorced, Sara had said she planned to change her will, giving it all to her environmental causes instead. She procrastinated. And now she's dead. How Adrienne found out about the will, I don't know. But there's her motive."

"Why would Adrienne hire me to uncover a murder she herself committed?" I tried to let on that I bought Parke's theory, hoping he'd give me more.

"To point suspicion at me." Parke thumped his fat index finger repeatedly into his chest.

"But she hadn't even seen Sara for years."

"If you believe anything Adrienne Ridgely says, you can't be much of a detective."

fifteen

"Greg Parke is a pathological liar." Adrienne bristled. "I told you not to believe anything he said about me."

"Is he wrong?" I aimed my Impala up the Pali Highway the next morning, heading for Sara's beach house in Lanikai. "Did your falling out with Sara have anything to do with a man in Boston?"

"We had a disagreement. You knew that before you interviewed Greg."

"Was the disagreement over Sara's fiancé?"

"I can't listen to Greg's lies about me," she fumed. "You can believe him, or you can believe me."

We cleared the Pali tunnels and began weaving down to the windward side.

"To do the job you hired me for, Adrienne, there are some things I need to know." I glanced at her face, which was set in a rigid expression. "Parke claims Sara was about to change her will before she died, to cut you out completely. What about it?"

Adrienne was silent for a minute. "No, I didn't know. I suppose Greg thinks Sara's money should have gone back to him?"

"No, he says she planned to donate it to her causes."

Adrienne shifted in her seat. "So was your whole conversation centered on me, or did you find out anything about Greg?"

Was she being evasive or straightforward? I decided to give her the benefit of the doubt.

"Parke admitted knowing both Heather Linborg and Milton Yu. And he confessed to going to Kalaupapa to find Sara. He says he was still in love with her, though he claims she cheated on him."

"Sara cheated?"

"Parke even gave me a name."

"Who?"

"The man you just had dinner with. Rush McWhorter."

Adrienne turned from me and gazed silently at pale Kailua Bay.

When we reached Lanikai, I pulled into a gravel drive at the quiet, cul-de-sac end of the beach. Sara had spent a sizable chunk of her divorce settlement on two adjacent oceanfront lots shaded by coconut palms. Combined, they contained only one small cottage, which most new owners in her shoes would have torn down and replaced with a massive castle covering every available inch of land. I credited Sara for trying to retain the property's natural beauty.

The cottage itself was rustic and charming: shake roof, stone fireplace, hardwood floors, two cozy bedrooms, a *koa*-paneled study overlooking the twin Mokulua Islands, and a small kitchen—the total opposite of her ex-husband's Kāhala mansion.

I'd suggested we come here in search of more clues about Sara's talk at the health food store, or her connections to any of the witnesses. We focused first on Sara's study. Adrienne sorted through papers in Sara's rolltop desk. I worked my way through her filing drawers. Just as I started on the second drawer, Adrienne waved a torn sheet of yellow legal paper. "Look at this!"

"What is it?"

"An itinerary."

Written in Sara's hand, the itinerary listed her activities on Moloka'i that fateful day. The notes revealed she had planned to tour Kalaupapa, then to speak that night in Kaunakakai, at Sun Whole Foods as Yu had told me. The title of the Sara's talk was to be "Stop Kalaupapa Cliffs!"

"It's our lucky day," Adrienne said.

"If we can find a copy of her speech," I said. "Or did she write down her speeches?

"I have no idea.

We searched every drawer and stack of papers, but found nothing. As the morning grew on, we decided to switch tactics and visit the U.H. Law School, where Sara taught—and where she likely had a computer we could search. My curiosity was piqued by Parke's allegations of infidelity by his former wife, so I had already arranged to interview Rush McWhorter there at noon.

As we drove onto the Mānoa Valley campus, I recalled a retired professor telling me about a time when these grounds were once as pristine and garden-like as the misted valley that provides its spectacular backdrop. Another victim of overdevelopment, the university was now choked with mismatched buildings: plantation-era cottages with buzzing air conditioners, cement-slab shoe boxes from the 1950s, stark, avant-garde towers circa 1960s, and an art deco student center in mauve and hunter green. As my eye glanced from one façade to another, diverse architectural styles clashed.

In the sparse lower campus, on the edge of a defunct quarry, stood the bunker-like complex of the law school. Inside we easily found the door we were looking for: "Sara Ridgely-Parke, Assoc. Prof." A month after her death, the office still bore Sara's name.

"They're waiting for me to clear it out," Adrienne said, unlocking the door and pushing it open.

The office had one sealed window overlooking Waikīkī and that musty smell that accumulated paper always takes on in the Islands' damp air. I imagined Sara glancing from her office window at the ragged skyline of concrete, steel, and glass—the symbol of paved-over paradise—and renewing her resolve to fight overdevelopment. I couldn't fully buy Parke's description of Sara being so like him that she embraced the luxuries that development brought. Her life's work spoke too loudly for itself.

Scanning her office, I saw creative clutter everywhere: open files and law books, papers hastily arranged on the floor, colored sticky notes tacked up like Christmas cards, newspaper articles taped to the walls. One article discussed the re-interment at Kalaupapa of Blessed Father Damien's right hand, considered a holy relic. The most prominent clipping, titled "Chancellor Trust Plans 'Kalaupapa Cliffs' Resort," echoed the sketch I had first seen on the airplane on my way to Moloka'i.

We searched for a hard copy of Sara's speech without success, but we did find two class rosters that included the name of missing fisherman, Baron Taniguchi. Adrienne agreed to keep hunting for the speech while I met with McWhorter at the other end of the hall.

Russell T. McWhorter taught real estate law and was well-connected with both developers and politicians in a state where the two went hand-in-hand. Since government approvals were required to get any construction project off the ground, a developer would often share his or her spoils with key politicians. An investment group would then be formed called a *hui,* a partnership with all the influential players, even sometimes underworld types who funneled in ill-gotten dollars. Whenever an approval was required, the project would slide through slick as grease.

The door opened to a rod-straight man in his thirties with a well-rehearsed smile and darting eyes of drab olive. His pale blonde hair was cropped fashionably close, nearly shaved at the temples like a marine cut. McWhorter was rough-hewn handsome and wore the silk aloha shirt of a downtown banker.

He gestured woodenly toward a visitor's chair. Despite a No Smoking sign posted in the hall outside his door, on McWhorter's desk sat a pack of Marlboro Lights and an ashtray full of butts. I handed him my card as he positioned himself behind his wide desk. His stiffness and tight smile didn't make me feel very welcome.

He glanced at my card. "Quite a gimmick. That 'Surfing Detective' bit. You must get some interesting cases."

"True." I wondered if he was mocking me.

"Do you actually surf?" he asked in a voice thinner than his rugged "Marlboro Man" image suggested.

"When time allows."

"A dangerous sport." McWhorter smirked. "So you came to talk about Sara?" He wasted few words.

"Yes, I'm investigating the professor's death on Moloka'i."

"Adrienne mentioned it." McWhorter reached for his pack of Marlboros. "Want one?" He flashed the flip-top box.

"No, thanks."

"Sara's passing was a shock to everyone here." He pulled out a cigarette, then flicked his lighter. A tongue of yellow flame licked out. "I'm not surprised Adrienne hired you to investigate the accident, given her emotional state." He took a long drag, then exhaled a grey cloud. "But I seriously doubt her theory that Sara's fall was somehow arranged."

"I'm just doing my job." I said.

He took another drag from his smoke. "Sara was truly an exceptional woman and a top-notch attorney. We'd all like to bring her back."

"Your reflections on her career might benefit the investigation. First, do you know this missing law student, Baron Taniguchi?"

"Taniguchi?" McWhorter blew another grey plume. "Why?"

"Curiosity. His disappearance has been so much in the news."

"Baron took one class from me." McWhorter flicked his cigarette ash. "He did well. That's all I remember about him."

"Real estate law is your specialty?" I knew the answer, but wanted to keep him talking.

McWhorter nodded as he puffed on his cigarette, the air in his office becoming thick. "I also advise the Chancellor Trust on real estate matters."

"Representing the trust must have put you at odds with Sara."

"I admired Sara even though, politically speaking, we were on opposite sides of the fence. She opposed developing the islands, and took her opposition to extremes."

"What extremes?"

"Once on ABC's 'Nightline' she called Waikīkī a 'high-rise horror.' The tourism board did backflips!" McWhorter puffed. "'No building taller than a coconut palm.' That was Sara's slogan. She'd have us all living on the beach in little grass shacks."

"Interesting idea."

"Pure nostalgia. No sane person in Hawai'i today believes we can go back to that . . ."

The more McWhorter talked, the more I wondered how Sara could have found him at all attractive. Despite his rugged good looks and practiced smile, rigidity seemed to fix his character, from his stiff posture to his abrupt dismissal of those who held opinions different than his own.

"Development means jobs," McWhorter continued. "Sara forgot working people when she married Gregory Parke and moved to Kāhala."

What a smoke screen. McWhorter struck me as someone who couldn't care less about the average Joe or Jane.

"Does it seem strange to you that Sara married Parke?"

"Sara lost her senses for a while." McWhorter tapped off another glowing ash. "But at least she recovered and divorced him."

"Because she was in love with you?" I went out on a limb.

McWhorter's eyes widened. "What kind of question is that?"

"Just something I heard." I kept my gaze level.

"From whom?" The attorney peered at me through the haze. "Was it Adrienne?"

"No, not Adrienne."

"I'm surprised." He blew another cloud and frowned. "She knows me better than she'll probably admit."

His remark jarred me, but I tried not to show it. "How much better?"

"She's your client." He put on a tight smile again. "Why don't you ask her?"

sixteen

I marched back into Sara's office, steaming. "Tell me everything about you and Rush McWhorter," I said to Adrienne, trying to hold back my anger.

"Rush and me?" Adrienne tried to act incredulous. "What do you mean?"

"You know him better than you've said, according to McWhorter."

"Not this again." Her steely eyes pierced me like daggers.

"Not what again?"

"You're believing somebody else's word more than mine."

"Only when you don't tell me everything. Only when you leave out huge chunks about Sara or yourself, which seems to be happening often."

"All right, I knew Rush before."

"For how long?"

Adrienne glanced away. "About six years."

Now it was my turn to be incredulous. "You knew him even before your sister came to Hawai'i?"

"Sara was engaged to Rush in Boston."

"So he's the man you stole from Sara?"

"I didn't *steal* anyone," she said. "After Rush and Sara became engaged, he took an interest in me. I tried not to encourage him."

"Nonetheless, it nixed Sara's wedding plans."

"Their marriage wasn't meant to be. But after Rush left Sara, she wouldn't speak to me. It was horrible. Eventually I broke off with Rush."

"Then McWhorter suddenly wanted your sister again?"

"Yes, that's why he came to Hawai'i. Rush applied for a teaching job at the law school and was hired, but Sara would hardly speak to him after what happened in Boston."

"That's when she married Parke?"

"Rush hounded her with proposals. I think she married Greg, in part, to discourage Rush."

I couldn't believe she had been concealing this potentially major point of relevance. "Why didn't you tell me this before?"

"I didn't feel the need to reveal my personal life. Sara is our focus here."

"If Parke would kill your sister over jealously of McWhorter, then our focus just expanded. Have you ever considered suspecting McWhorter himself? Maybe jealously could have led him to revenge, too?"

"Inconceivable. Rush was mad about Sara. Always has been. Now if we can stop the interrogation for a moment, I have something to show you." Adrienne pulled a yellow legal pad from the bottom drawer of Sara's desk. "It was hidden in this tablet."

"You found the speech?"

Adrienne handed me the yellow pad. Sara had slipped each white page of her speech between as many yellow leaves in the legal pad, making the typescript virtually disappear.

"She must have thought someone was snooping on her," Adrienne said.

I liberated the first typed page from the pad. What Adrienne had found was probably a late or final draft, since the copy was clean and the speech appeared to be fully developed. In the upper left-hand corner Sara had typed the place and date: Sun Whole Foods, Kaunakakai. Wed., September 6. The day she died.

Adrienne moved closer to me and began to read:

Stop Kalaupapa Cliffs!

It's a pleasure to see so many old friends here tonight from the coalition against Chancellor Trust's proposed Kalaupapa Cliffs resort. You deserve heartfelt thanks for your grit and your perseverance. Already you have succeeded in mobilizing grassroots opposition. And by now you know what you are up against. I'm here this evening to offer you encouragement in your battle. But more important, I bring ammunition to help you win . . .

"That sounds like Sara," Adrienne said. "Always a fighter."

Few people realize what it's like to face off against a billion-dollar trust. Their fleet of lawyers can file endless injunctions, restraining orders, and suits against you; their friends at all levels of government – from the governor's office to the legislature to the courts – can put roadblocks at your every turn; their massive publicity and disinformation engines can smear and malign you. In sum, this Goliath has enormous power to intimidate and impede you through all these channels and more.

The single largest private landholder in Hawai'i, the Chancellor Trust owns, by some estimates, as much as 10 percent of the islands – more than the U.S. Government! The consequences of the Trust's real estate dominance have been devastating for most citizens. By hoarding immense tracts of land, the Trust – called by one economist a 'land oligopoly' – increases the already high cost of housing, pinching strapped island families. At the same time, its five trustees pay themselves annual salaries approaching a million dollars – each!

"Those salaries are notorious," I interrupted. "And the Trust calls itself a 'nonprofit' organization!"

Adrienne continued:

The Hawaiian people, whom the Trust was charged by the will of Marie Kaleilani Chancellor to aid, have too often fallen victim to its ambitions. You may recall an incident that happened in a peaceful valley in East O'ahu. To clear these remote and pristine acres for an immense housing track which would generate millions in profits, Chancellor Trust evicted several impoverished Hawaiian homesteaders in a confrontation so bitter it nearly ended in a shoot-out. The Hawaiians were driven from the land and some arrested. In their place the Trust constructed dozens of look-alike tract houses that those Hawaiians could not afford to buy, while enriching the Trust and forever altering the character of the once-tranquil valley.

Sara's speech made me recall my own silent support for those Hawaiian homesteaders. It had been a different era back then—before the rise of the Hawaiian sovereignty movement. The media had portrayed the embattled families as unfortunate impediments to progress, even as dangerous radicals. As Adrienne read on, I became curious as to Sara's promised "ammunition" against the Trust.

Chancellor Trust has now set its sights on Kalaupapa and the wishes of the Hawaiian people apparently matter little to the trustees. How large is the proposed "Kalaupapa Cliffs"? Kaunakakai, the biggest town on your island, could easily fit inside it. Or, to compare it to a familiar fixture on O'ahu, massive Ala Moana Shopping Center would fill little more than half of the site, leaving room for another medium-sized mall.

But why would Chancellor Trust invest so much of its own money in the sleepy island of Moloka'i? Why build a resort on a windswept, rainy cliff, when sunny beaches can be had on this and other islands?

The answer is simple: Blessed Father Damien will likely attain sainthood soon. His sanctification coupled with the adoption of Kalaupapa by the U.S. Park Service – and the certainty that the peninsula will become a full-fledged national park when the last remaining leprosy patients pass on – can mean only one thing: Tourism with a capital "T." Visitors from around the world, with religious pilgrims in the vanguard, will make this historic spot as populous as Lourdes.

There's only one hitch.   The project cannot go forward unless the state Land Zoning Board redesignates the land from "conservation" to "urban." In the current political climate, with heightened environmental awareness and sensitivity to Hawaiian history and culture, such a redesignation, you might assume, would be unthinkable. Indeed, your coalition survey found that 94 percent of Moloka'i residents oppose the project.

The trustees have anticipated public pressure on the Land Zoning Board to deny the trust's request, and they have concocted a secret plan to overcome it. This secret plan has been uncovered by a courageous volunteer, who revealed it to me at his peril. Although he must remain anonymous for his own safety, we have him to thank for this potent weapon against the trust . . .

The tie-in with Baron Taniguchi was now more than a hunch. He must have received tips on the Good Government Hotline, then passed them on, against protocol, to his esteemed mentor at the law school. For this plucky act, the avid fisherman had probably wound up as fish food.

To win approval for its project over stiff, broad-based opposition, the trust has formed a clandestine *hui* consisting of several state legislators, the spouse of a Land Zoning Board member, a development firm

partially owned by the lieutenant governor, the leader
of a hotel workers union, a legendary Hawaiian pop
singer, and even reputed underworld figures who will
funnel illegally obtained moneys into the project. This
hui includes the most influential, wealthy, and powerful
players in the islands, as well as Indonesian developer,
Umbro Zia.

Zia's name kept popping up. I had once seen a rare photo
of him in *Hawai'i Business News.* The reclusive billionaire had
been spotted in his trademark white suit and pale lavender
button-down shirt, a young Asian beauty at his side. Zia had
acquired his fortune through hit-and-run developments, mostly
sprawling shopping malls, in locales in which he never lived,
some say never set foot in. Before the last brick or tile was
cemented into place, Zia would be off to his next project, and
to the next after that. He was thus a fitting centerpiece of the
Chancellor Trust *hui*

Since Land Zoning Board members are politically
appointed and frequently beholden to politicians and
their powerful friends, they are very susceptible
to the kind of influential *hui* that Zia and the trust
have assembled. Unless we act now to expose them,
on Friday, October 20, when the Land Zoning Board
makes its final recommendation on "Kalaupapa Cliffs,"
the outcome is inevitable.

That was exactly one week from today. Adrienne continued
by reading the long list of names involved in the *hui*—a virtual
"who's who" of Hawai'i. I wasn't surprised to hear Rush

McWhorter's name, although Adrienne seemed to be, as she winced as her rollcall came to him. But I was floored when I heard the name of one of my very own *hānai* relatives–Uncle Manny, known to most as the famous Hawaiian pop singer Manny Lee. Never had I found myself so personally entwined with a client's case.

Not one of Sara's fellow mule riders made the list. Though if the *hui* was behind Sara's death, they most likely wouldn't send one of their own to do the dirty work. Rather, an unknown operative would be dispatched. So that didn't rule out the four witnesses. That Parke's name was also missing didn't mean he wasn't involved. As a big-time developer, he certainly had ties to the major players. And since Parke had shown me all the marks of a bitter, spurned ex-husband, a crime of passion still could not be ruled out.

At the conclusion of the speech, Sara revealed that she and her unnamed source had received death threats. Adrienne's eyes were beginning to tear as she handed the speech to me. Now there was no doubt. For the first time since Adrienne had stepped into my office with her bizarre murder theory, I was convinced we had a case.

seventeen

I suggested dinner that night at a Thai Restaurant in Waikīkī, and Adrienne agreed. She seemed to have dropped the cool act she was putting on after our night at the Halekūlani. But we kept the conversation on business. And, for better or worse, there were no Chi Chis on the menu here.

After dinner, Adrienne insisted on walking back to the Halekūlani, a half mile distance, alone. I sensed that this was her way of signaling the evening was over.

"Let me drive you. You shouldn't be walking alone at night." By now I had poked around enough in this case to know that whoever had killed Sara might be on to me—*and* Adrienne.

"Really, Kai! I'm accustomed to taking care of myself."

"Then give me a call when you get back to your hotel. O.K.?" I wrote my home phone number on the back of my business card and gave it to her.

She nodded grudgingly and turned with a wave of her hand.

When I got back to my apartment a while later, my phone message light was blinking. I pressed Play.

"Naughty surfer boy. Why haven't you called me?" Niki.

I almost tossed her photo off my *lānai*, a forty-five-story plunge to the sidewalk below. Suddenly I had a better idea. Removing Niki's picture from the nightstand, I pried open the retaining clips behind the frame, took off the cardboard backing, then slipped in Sara's speech, which had been folded in my shirt pocket. I replaced the backing and wiped the frame and glass. For the time being, Niki would provide a safe hiding place for my only hard evidence.

In bed that night above the murmur of the *Late Show*, I pondered the case. I began thinking more about one of the names on Sara's infamous list—Rush McWhorter. The two apparently had known a long, complex, and vexed relationship. How had it all played out? McWhorter's failed romance and his work for Chancellor Trust must have put him at constant loggerheads with the "ecofeminist" he once—and perhaps still—loved. Did Rush keep his distance or continue to pursue her? Did he become a more aggressive adversary? If so, he would have been in a perfect position to snoop on his colleague, considering the proximity of their offices and the fact that their computers were hooked to the same university mainframe.

Her computer. I decided to have another look at Sara's office in the morning. I switched off the television and tried to sleep. But something was bothering me.

Adrienne had not called.

I sat up and switched on the light. Dialing her number, I tried to estimate how long the walk would take. The phone kept ringing. She might not necessarily be back yet, and she'd probably think I was neurotic if I left a message. As she reminded me, she could take care of herself. I hung up the phone and tried to get some sleep.

The next morning I returned to the Mānoa campus and Sara's office. A key Adrienne had provided me opened the outside door of the office building, as well as Sara's own office. A quick look inside told me something wasn't right. Papers, files, notebooks, journals, pens, pencils—everything— lay essentially where they had been the day before, but the relationships among things looked different. Someone had been here. I checked the door for evidence of a break-in. No marks on the sill or the lock, though janitors' passkeys were easy enough to come by.

I wondered what had been taken. The most important document, Sara's speech, was safely tucked away in my apartment. And, of the suspects, only Milton Yu let on that he knew anything about it. A break-in seemed ill-timed—more than a month after Sara's death. What would be the point?

I turned on Sara's computer and scanned her many files, coming up with virtually nothing. Had the break-in artists cleared all incriminating files from her hard drive? I thought a minute. If there were any pertinent documents left, they were probably hiding in her email account since it would be more difficult to crack. Fortunately, I had learned how to circumvent the university's log-on and password requirements from an appreciative client who also happened to be a university computer science major.

Once in Sara's account, the computer flashed a message: "You Have New Mail." There were seventy-four new messages. About fifty appeared to be junk email and several were departmental memos addressed to all law faculty. A few looked personal. I noted one in particular dated the day before Sara died from baron@hotline.org, whom I assumed was Baron Taniguchi.

Sara,

Another threat came in today on the Hotline, this one aimed at you and me both. Be careful. I've never taken threats seriously before, but these *hui* guys sound serious.

I hope your Moloka'i mule ride pays off. What a clever way to let the folks at Kalaupapa know what Chancellor Trust is up to. Please give my regards to the folks at Sun Whole Foods. I'm sure your speech will galvanize the coalition.

The pressure of this trust business is getting to me. Only one way to handle it – night fishing at Bamboo Ridge!

Have a safe trip to Moloka'i.

Aloha,
Baron

I double-clicked on her Saved Messages folder, but before I could open any my solitude was disturbed.

Tap. Tap. Tap, A heavy hand rapped on the door. "Campus Secur-ah-tee," intoned a husky pidgin voice.

I rose from the desk and unlocked the door. A meaty local man in a khaki uniform peered in. He looked more like a heavy-weight wrestler than a security guard. I noticed his uniform displayed no official badges or patches.

"Wassup?" I asked in my best pidgin.

"Dis' professor Ridgely-Parke's office." He eyed me suspiciously. "What you doing hea?"

"Da Professor *go hala*," I replied. "She's dead."

"Know dat awready," said the man. "What you doing hea?"

"Work fo' da professor's family." I reached into my wallet and handed him my card.

He studied the surfer logo, then put the card in his shirt pocket. "O.K., brah." He turned and walked away.

Closing Sara's office door, I had second thoughts about giving the man my card. But it was too late now.

Turning back to Sara's saved messages, I found several more emails from Taniguchi in which he revealed the names of the *hui* members that Sara was going to expose to the public in her speech. If the *hui* had hacked into Taniguchi's e-mails, they would have known everything—including Baron's and Sara's whereabouts to arrange for their elimination.

These emails made it clear that Sara owed Taniguchi a great debt. He was the unsung hero of the coalition against Kalaupapa Cliffs. But now with Sara dead and the law student missing, only two people remained alive who knew of the undelivered speech and the identities of every *hui* member.

Adrienne and me.

eighteen

I found a floppy disk in Sara's desk and copied all the emails from Taniguchi. I then shut down Sara's computer and left her office, locking the door behind me. I had the eerie feeling of being watched. At the end of the darkened hall, the security guard in khakis stood eyeing me.

Chicken skin. He got my adrenaline pumping, as I quickly exited the front doors.

I steered my Impala down Beretania toward Maunakea Street. After less than a mile, a smoke grey Dodge van suddenly appeared in my rearview mirror. It kept behind me for several miles—about ten car lengths back. By the time I turned onto Maunakea, the van was gone.

I pulled up to my office building and found Mrs. Fujiyama doing a brisk business inside the flower shop on this Saturday morning. The color and scent of freshly strung *lei* filled the bustling shop—orange *'ilima,* pale yellow plumeria, lavender crown flowers, fire red *lehua,* green *maile* leaves, pink rosebuds. Their sweet aroma compensated in some way for this foul business I'd gotten involved in.

I wove around several customers, nodded to Chastity, the *lei* girl, and hurried up the stairs. Only one other office tenant was in today, Madame Zenobia, the psychic. Behind her psychedelic bead curtain flickered a single candle. Incense wafted into the hallway as a musty haze. Perched on a throne-like wicker chair amidst the smoke, Madame whispered tremulously in her bejeweled turban. A shriveled woman with blue hair sat across from her, glued to every word.

"I see a messenger bearing bad tidings," the medium told her client. "For the rest of this day, do not answer your door. Do not pick up your phone. Respond to no one. With vigilance, the danger will pass."

The blue-haired woman nodded slowly, entranced.

I reached the familiar surfer on my office door, the thick mahogany and twin dead bolts so reassuring. Inside, on my desk, sat the same stack of invoices and bills that should have been filed last week, or the week before. It didn't take long to save on my computer's hard drive the vital files from Sara's office.

As I was ejecting her floppy disk, my phone rang. I let it ring twice, then three times. For some reason I hesitated. Was I thinking of Madame Zenobia's warning? I let it ring a fourth time. Just before my answering machine kicked in, I lifted the receiver.

"You are the 'Surfing Detective,' yes?" asked a Middle Eastern male voice.

"I'm Kai Cooke." *Another crank call?*

"Mr. Cooke, I am Dr. Majerian, emergency room surgeon at Halekōkua Medical Center. You would kindly assist us, please, in locating the next of kin of a mainland accident victim?"

"Actually, I'm kind of busy with a case right now, but I can give you the name of another investigator."

"You, Mr. Cooke, I called first," the doctor continued, "because in her purse the victim had your business card. Last evening she was struck by a hit-and-run driver in Waikīkī"

"Waikīkī?"

"Correct, Sir."

"Not Adrienne?"

"Yes, her Massachusetts driver's license says 'Adrienne M. Ridgely.'"

No words would come.

"Mr. Cooke? . . . Hello?"

I bolted out the door.

My Impala ripped along King Street at double the speed limit, through three yellow lights and one red. I squealed left against another red light at Punahou Street, then sped *mauka* up the hill toward the slopes of Tantalus. Just before the H-1 overpass, I screeched to the curb in front of Halekōkua Medical Center.

I ran to the emergency room and asked the first green smock I saw where I could find Adrienne. The orderly sent me to the ER admissions desk, where a receptionist sat behind a computer. She typed in Adrienne's name and gazed at the screen.

"ICU," she said. "Ms. Ridgely came out of surgery early this morning."

"ICU?" I asked, breathless from my run.

"Intensive care. Her surgeon was Dr. Majerian."

"Could you please page the doctor? Tell him it's Kai Cooke. He's expecting me."

I stood huffing by the desk with my arms folded while she paged. "Dr. Majerian, call ER reception . . ."

A few minutes that felt like hours passed. Then the phone rang. The receptionist answered in whispered tones I couldn't hear.

A minute later, a slight man with coffee-colored skin stepped off the elevator across the lobby and walked to the ER desk. His eyes were ebony and moist.

"How is Adrienne?" I asked.

He spoke softly: "Come, please, with me."

We rode the elevator up to the second floor. "On Lewers Street the police found her, yes, at about ten last night in Waikīkī," the doctor said. "From her purse was taken apparently nothing. Puzzling, no?"

"It was hit-and-run?"

Dr. Majerian nodded. He still hadn't told me Adrienne's condition. Now I was reluctant to ask.

We walked down a wide hallway ending at a pair of large double doors marked, Intensive Care–Medical Personnel Only. Dr. Majerian pushed through the doors into a big bay with several alcoves, each one holding a patient on a gurney surrounded by an awesome assemblage of high-tech medical machines. Nurses scurried from alcove to alcove. Patients were attached to the equipment through various tubes and lines and straps, like spacewalkers tethered to a mother ship. All looked utterly helpless. Ashen white, dependent for their existence on IV drips, oxygen hoses, tracheal tubes, and electronic hookups to measure heartbeat, pulse, blood pressure, body temperature.

It was a sobering sight. *No wonder the hospital doesn't let visitors in here.* I couldn't imagine Adrienne looking so defenseless.

"Please, this way . . ." Dr. Majerian walked on and I followed.

We approached a gurney holding another ashen creature. The same array of tubes connected this frail patient to the many machines, including a tracheal tube. She couldn't even breathe on her own. As Dr. Majerian scanned a clipboard at the foot of the gurney, I beheld the now-helpless woman from Boston who less than a week ago had made passionate love to me.

Gone was the color in her cheeks. Her skin looked not just pale, but paper white. She lay motionless except for the slow rise and fall of her chest. Those vivid grey-blue eyes now lay behind pale, closed lids. Her luxuriant chestnut hair appeared straw-like and was bloodied. She wore a plain smock, also blood splattered.

"She is in critical condition," the doctor said.

"What did she break?"

"Broken bones are not the problem, Mr. Cooke. The severe concussion, rather."

"Is she in a coma?"

"Later we will know. At present, she is still traumatized."

I watched Adrienne for any sign of life—the rustle of a limb, the blink of an eye, a sigh, a cough—anything.

"Mr. Cooke, sir," the doctor said. "Please, would you provide us with some information about her?"

"I'll tell you what I know."

I related to him the story of Adrienne coming into my office the week before and hiring me to investigate her sister's death on Moloka'i. I told him that both of Adrienne's parents were deceased, as well as her only sister, whose demise I was investigating. I frankly didn't know who he could contact in Boston. And while I did know one person who might tell us—McWhorter—I wasn't about to give his name to the doctor until I could be sure he wasn't responsible for this.

Dr. Majerian jotted a few things on his clipboard. Before he was finished, I swore I saw Adrienne move—a slight flutter of a finger. But I must have been dreaming.

"Did anyone see the car that hit her?" I asked.

"I do not believe so. The police, they may have more information on the accident."

This was no accident. I approached the gurney on which Adrienne lay and touched her cold hand.

"I'll be back for you," I whispered into her unhearing ear.

nineteen

During the two-mile trip from the hospital back to Maunakea Street, I again saw the van that had been tailing me the day before. When I turned *makai* onto Maunakea, the van turned, too. I swung into my garage and watched the van slowly pass and pull to the curb. I kept my eyes on the van for several minutes, then walked the back route to my office, using the side door on Beretania Street.

The monitor of my PC still glowed. I shut it down, then peeked out the window onto Maunakea Street. The van was gone.

My phone rang. This time I heeded Madame Zenobia's warning and didn't pick up. After four rings the answering machine answered.

"Mister Cooke, dis ist Docktor Otto Frenz. I haf found somet'ing about das mule vich may interest you. Only one case I find in der journals vhere das mule stumble ven not spooked or ill."

Dr. Frenz paused. I heard the sound of shuffling papers.

"Ya, here." He paused again, then apparently read from a journal.

"Ven mule ist sedated, if large dosage ist indicated, he mus' be allowt sufficient recovery time bevore valking again, since he may be drowsy und not sure of foot. Drugs, Mr. Cooke," Dr. Frenz concluded. "Das ist best I can do. *Auf Wiedersehen.*"

He hung up.

I played Dr. Frenz's message again, recalling Kaluna's comment about his fallen mule: Even though Coco's leg was broken, he had lain peacefully. Heather Linborg observed the same. The veterinarian provided an explanation for both why the animal had stumbled and why it did not suffer.

But how could Coco have been drugged under Kaluna's watchful eye? No *paniolo* would let his animal be so abused. There had to be more clues—on the trail, in Kaluapapa town. It looked like I would be paying another visit to Moloka'i.

Sunday morning I visited Adrienne again at the medical center. She had been moved from intensive care to a hospital room—a positive sign.

In place of her tracheal tube, an oxygen line now led to her nose from a spigot on the wall marked O_2. Adrienne looked much as she had the day before: eyes closed, hair lusterless and drawn back, skin paper white. She had not shown any sign of consciousness since her accident. I sat beside her for nearly an hour, watching the barely perceptible movement of her breath.

At about nine I left the silent Adrienne and headed back to my office with a growing sense of urgency. In some strange way, I felt Adrienne's recovery depended somehow on my solving her sister's murder. I checked the rearview mirror. No van. Since Adrienne's accident, I could feel the *hui* hovering everywhere.

Fujiyama's is closed on Sundays, but when I walked up to the building, one of the front doors on Maunakea was open. *Strange.* I saw Mrs. Fujiyama inside, head in her display cases, her half glasses riding low on her nose. She gazed up when I walked in.

"There's some bad people in this world, Mr. Cooke."

"Surprised to see you here on Sunday, Mrs. Fujiyama. What's wrong?"

"The police just left. Last night robbers broke in."

"What did they take?"

"Nothing," she said. "They took nothing."

"Are you sure?" I didn't like the sound of this.

She nodded. "Better check your office," she added. "The police said the robbers went upstairs, too."

I ran up the orange shag stairs, trying to reassure myself that my two dead bolts and solid mahogany door could keep out any intruder. The flimsy, hollow-core doors of the other four tenants were closed and locked. *No break-ins there.*

With relief, I saw that my own door was also closed tight. I put my key into the top lock, which opened with the usual click. But the second made a different sound.

The door swung open to an office in shambles. My file folders and their reams of client records lay scattered on the floor as if hit by a hurricane. My computer was gone, its unattached power line and printer cable resembling torn umbilical cords. And my tarnished longboard trophy had taken a dive, head first, into the wastebasket.

The *hui* was giving me a wake-up call. They had killed Sara. They had disappeared Baron Taniguchi. They had run down Adrienne. Now they were sending a message that they could do the same to me. How had they managed to break into my office without busting down the door, then trash the place and not get caught? I grudgingly gave credit to their techniques, then wondered if they had done the same to my apartment.

I closed up my ransacked office and drove to the Waikīkī Edgewater. Packing into an already-crowded elevator, I pushed PH. The ride to the penthouses seemed to take forever, the elevator stopping six or seven times on the forty-five floor climb. Finally, the doors opened to the familiar floor and I hurried down the hall.

My door appeared to be locked just as I had left it. The turning of my key produced no unusual sound.

Inside everything looked in place. I rushed straight to the nightstand and grabbed my photo of Niki, still beaming a heartbreaking smile in her string bikini. I inspected the photo, the glass, the frame, and the cardboard backing. From the thickness of the backing I could tell all was well.

Relieved, I immediately called Johnny Kaluna, who picked up on the first ring. Since the mule guide's tour business was still suspended, he had time on his hands and agreed to hike again with me down the Kalaupapa trail. I told him I was in a hurry. We settled on the next morning, Monday, at nine.

After I made reservations for my impromptu Moloka'i trip, I called the Halekōkua. No change in Adrienne's condition. I walked out on the lānai and leaned on the railing. The mid-afternoon sun was reflecting in brilliant patches off the distant ocean. I might as well go back to the office and deal with the mess there, since I couldn't bear the thought of coming home from Moloka'i to ankle-deep files.

But I knew it wasn't my files the *hui* had been after. It was my computer. All of Baron Taniguchi's transferred email files, incriminating *hui* members, were now lost.

twenty

After a bouncy but uneventful flight later that afternoon to Moloka'i, I picked up another rental car at the tiny airport and drove to Kaunakakai. On the edge of town I saw that white-muzzled retriever snoozing at Kalama's Service Station, then I passed Sun Whole Foods where Sara was to have delivered her speech.

I arrived at the 'Ukulele Inn at sunset. At the front desk, a Hawaiian woman in a tent-sized *mu'umu'u* checked me in.

"Room 21d," she said. "Sign da book, please?" She opened a spiral-bound register on the counter. It contained guests' names for each day of year.

I signed, then asked in pidgin: "O.K. I can look an' see if any my frien's stay here?"

"When your frien's come?"

"Septembah—I t'ink maybe foah, five, maybe six."

"*Huli* da page." She made a page-turning gesture.

I turned the log back to "September 4," two days before Sara's death. I scanned the register. Among perhaps thirty autographs, I could decipher none of my suspects' names.

"You fine 'em yet?"

"Looking." Toward the bottom of the page, I squinted to read a tightly scrawled name: "J. G. Parke."

I tried to conceal my glee. "Maybe try da next page, too." Among the many names on the page dated September 5, was "H. Linborg" in a swooping, feminine hand.

"Find your frien'?"

"No can find." I attempted to keep a straight face. "Try one more page."

I turned to September 6, the day of Sara's fall. Three dozen names appeared, but no suspects, unless they had used aliases.

"Shoots. No luck."

"Maybe dey stay anoddah hotel?" she suggested.

"Where you t'ink?"

"Try Moloka'i Beach Hotel. Ask for my frien' in reservations, Mele."

"T'anks, eh?"

Within minutes, my rented car was flying two miles up shore to the Moloka'i Beach Hotel. I wandered among its Polynesian thatched cottages, soon coming upon an open-air lobby flanked by two towering *koa* statues—*ki'i* or tiki—apparently of local gods.

The reservationist I had been instructed to see, Mele, showed me the guest register for September 3 through 7. I scanned the pages for suspects Goto, Yu, Archibald, and McWhorter. Only Archibald's name appeared, on September 4 in a beachfront cottage. Listed in the same room with Archibald was another guest named Stevens.

The travel agent had lied, claiming to have journeyed to Moloka'i alone. I suppose if the *hui* had wanted a remote hit man with little obvious local connection, Archibald or this

Stevens could have been their man—or woman. I asked if the receptionist could tell me more about the mysterious traveling companion. Was Stevens also a travel agent? Did the two check in together? Did they take meals together?

Mele didn't know. But she told me to come back on Sunday to talk to someone who might, a chambermaid named Raine who cleaned the seaside cottages.

After grilled *mahimahi* that evening at the 'Ukulele Inn, I stopped by the Banyan Tree. The same local surfer was tending bar as before.

"Hey, Kai, wassup?" he said.

I ordered a beer and put another ten on the bar. "Keep da change."

"T'anks, eh." He set a frothing mug in front of me and picked up the bill.

We talked story about surfing for a while, then I steered our conversation toward the case.

"Eh, brah, you remembah dis' guy?" I showed him the photo of Parke. "Was here 'bout one mont' ago. One *haole* guy, mid-fifties."

The bartender studied the photo. "Ho, how can I forget! I wen' see him sitting wit' one *ono wahine*."

"You remembah what da *wahine* look like?"

He smiled wistfully. "Was blon'. I t'ink she one masseuse, or somet'ing. *Lomilomi* kine."

"Was named Heather?"

"Maybe. Dey wen' meet in da bar and lef' togeddah. Dat's her style. I seen her operate hea befoah."

"She one hooker?"

The bartender shrugged his shoulders. "I dunno. Maybe. I no ask."

"Why you t'ink she work hea on Moloka'i? Brah, t'ink she no get plenny business on Maui?"

"Maybe she no like nobody fin' out."

"Like her boss?" I thought out loud. "Or maybe she get one boyfriend?"

"I dunno, brah. Whatevahs."

"T'anks, eh." I clasped his hand. "If you t'ink of anyt'ing else, try call me, 'kay?" I handed him my card.

Back in my room I mulled over our conversation. Heather was indeed in "the business." And as I assumed all along, she too had lied. She did know Parke. Intimately. Maybe she needed the money. Or maybe she was working for somebody else . . . A pimp. A crime syndicate. The *hui* itself.

I climbed into bed. The Spartan accommodations—no TV, no radio, no clock—hardly mattered this time. Morning was on my mind. Tomorrow I had a murder to solve.

twenty-one

"Errr-Errr-Erroooo!"

The ruby red rooster that struts the grounds at the 'Ukulele Inn crowed like clockwork before six the next morning.

I turned over in my bed, too groggy to rise. Last night the bar band had played Jimmy Buffet tunes until past midnight— evidently my room wasn't far enough away to block the sound. Then some rowdy and tone-deaf merrymakers in a nearby room had sung "Margaritaville" off-key for who knows how long. I would have had a rough night anyway. My thoughts kept returning to the Halekōkua Medical Center. Adrienne was in a coma and I felt responsible.

On the way to my meeting with Kaluna, I stopped at Kanemitsu Bakery, where I sipped Kona coffee and turned over details of the case. None of my theories were going to matter much without hard evidence. With a loaf of freshly-baked Moloka'i bread in hand, I headed up the two-lane highway to the cliffs of Kalaupapa.

A few miles from the summit, mist clouded my windshield, then cleared as the sun emerged. I passed the countless acres of conservation land Chancellor Trust proposed to plow under, where *kukui* and ironwood trees waved in the cool morning trade winds. The Land Zoning Board was expected to approve the project on Friday—just four days away.

I pulled up to the mule stable a few minutes early. The corral, as before, lay empty. Inside the barn the wooden feeding troughs still held no feed. Saddles, blankets, harnesses, bits—all the riding gear—hung as before, awaiting the animals' return. The barn was ghostly quiet, except for a hen pecking by the troughs where once seeds and morsels of food had been.

In what mood had Sara waited here before her fateful ride? Was she on guard, alarmed by the death threats against her? Or was she at ease, having escaped, if briefly, to the more pristine Hawai'i she was fighting to preserve?

I wandered outside to the corral, just as Kaluna's Jeep rattled into view. He hopped out in his signature black felt cowboy hat and worn denims, then ambled toward me in the elegantly bowlegged walk of a *paniolo.*

He extended his hand. "Kai, *aloha mai.*"

"I brought you one small *makana.*" From my car I fetched the gift—warm bread from Kanemitsu Bakery.

"Oh *mahalo.*" He breathed in the fresh-baked aroma. "We no get dis' kine bread up hea."

"I pay fo' da hike today, like da last time."

"*Mahalo,* Kai." Kaluna smiled. "Your client still not satisfy 'bout da accident?"

"My client in da hospital. Was run down I t'ink by da same *hui* dat kill da *wahine.*"

"Nobody kill da *wahine,*" Kaluna shook his head. "Coco wen' stumble."

"But Kaluna, you say yourself it no like Coco fo' stumble. You say, 'Coco one good mule.'"

"*'Ae,* real good."

"Well den, somebody wen' mess wit' Coco."

"Nobody mess wit' Coco," Kaluna protested. "Nobody go neah da mules but me and da customahs. And I dere wit' Coco da whole time."

"Da whole time? You sure?"

"All da time 'cept when da customahs take da walking tour down dere in Kalaupapa . . ." Kaluna paused. "Den Coco tether wit' da oddah mules and I talk story wit' some friens'."

"One vet in Waimānalo t'ink Coco drugged."

"Coco drug'?" Kaluna's leathery face contorted. "*'A'ole!* Nevah!"

"Maybe one customah give Coco drugs when you wen' talk story."

The mule guide ripped off his cowboy hat and grimaced again. "One customah drug Coco?"

"Is jus' one t'eory, but if we fin' evidence, your company get plenny *kālā*–plenny money."

"How?" The *paniolo* restored his hat.

"Ask your lawyers. Dey sue da guilty party fo' cause da accident and fo' damage your business. Da court award millions in case like dis."

"Millions?" Kaluna's brown eyes widened.

I pulled out my wallet. "I pay now fo' da hike."

Kaluna waved me off. "We fine dat drug evidence, Kai, an' you no owe me nut'ing."

We crossed the highway and walked down the winding red dirt road that led to the Kalaupapa trail. On my previous trip, this panoramic view of the tiny colony and leaf-shaped peninsula had been shrouded in mist. Today, under the bright October sun, every detail was sharply etched like a picture postcard. The waves washing the chocolate beach below were brilliant turquoise. The whipped cream foam looked good enough to eat. Above on the ridge a gentle breeze whispered in the ironwoods, carrying a fresh scent that stirred my senses.

I recalled the fabled motto of Kalaupapa: *'A'ole kānā wai ma kēia wahi*—"In this place there is no law." The saying was old, dating back to the nineteenth century, but its meaning had carried forward with a new twist. I glanced toward the eighty acres that Chancellor Trust, allied with a "who's who" of Hawai'i leaders, was poised to desecrate. Who would have dreamt that the lawless of today would be our own public officials sworn to uphold the law?

Before we started down the trail, Kaluna stopped at the grave of his fallen mule, marked by that pine cross with the crudely carved "Coco." Kaluna gazed at the cross. The red earth beneath it, once mounded high on the immense plot, already looked sunken like a little valley.

"If da mule nevah cause da accident," Kaluna said, pausing at the grave, then fixing his glistening brown eyes me, "I like clear Coco's name. Let's *hele!*"

We hiked through the first few canopied switchbacks, nearly every turn bringing breathtaking views of the wave-pounded peninsula. In the open stretches, the sweltering sun beat down, but to our great advantage: No rain-slick boulders or gooey red mud to challenge our footing today.

About halfway down the trail we began to hear the quiet wash of surf. At the red "15" marker, beneath the site of proposed Kalaupapa Cliffs resort, we made a sharp left to the rocky path from which Sara had fallen. I glanced down and involuntarily took a deep breath, envisioning Sara's slight body being thrown from her mule, lunging over the edge, clutching the air in a futile attempt to regain a hold on life before gravity dashed it from her on the rocks below.

I glanced back at the pockmarked trail. In the last month, mist and rain had washed the boulders and red earth. The searing sun had baked the crusty soil. I searched the accident site as before but, not surprisingly, came up empty.

Before turning at "16," we paused again at the flat-topped boulder with the makeshift shrine—Madonna, baby Jesus, wise men, *maile lei,* and rosary beads. The huddled, tiny figurines looked both sorrowful and jubilant. Despair and hope—two opposite emotions—portrayed in the same poignant scene. I noticed that atop the boulder the two red roses we had seen before were gone. In their place lay a fresh new rose, crimson and fragrant. Someone had recently—very recently—tended this shrine. I looked at Kaluna, who crossed himself as we passed. Then his eyes met mine.

"Fo' Coco and da *wahine.*" He walked on.

The trail seesawed down through the remaining switchbacks, the village of Kalaupapa growing under my gaze—from a grid of tiny specks to visible outlines of frame houses and gardens. Every so often I spotted a glinting object—a bottle cap, a plastic spoon, a piece of rusty pipe that recalled earlier days when mules ferried Kalaupapa's basic supplies. Around each object I scoured the trail with a falcon-like, circular search pattern, combing every inch of accessible ground on and off the trail. Nothing. In some places where the cliff dropped off too steeply, my search covered the narrow footpath alone. Still nothing.

Kaluna and I marched silently, scanning the trail as we covered the remaining few hundred feet. At the last switchback before Kalaupapa, the *paniolo* broke the silence.

"Eh, Kai, try look ovah deah. You see dat t'ing?" He pointed to a faint gleam about five strides off the trail. "What dat?"

I followed his finger, squatting to get a better look. The dully glimmering object lay on rocky soil under thick dwarf *kiawe,* so dense we would have to crawl on our bellies to fetch it.

I squinted to bring the subject into focus. "Look like one plastic bag reflecting da sun."

"I go take one closah look." Kaluna stepped off the trail.

"Might only be *'ōpala*—trash." I got down on my hands and knees. "But we no can afford to pass up nut'ing."

Kaluna stopped me. "I go."

"What fo'? Have to slither like one gecko under dat brush."

"*'A'ole pilikia*—no problem. I do it for Coco."

Kaluna crouched down and crawled. His black felt cowboy hat flopped off under the first low *kiawe* branch. He kept crawling until he was out of sight except for his well-worn boot soles. I remembered I had brought my camera and snapped a few pictures, in case this led to the discovery of evidence we might use.

Suddenly a long, slithering insect darted toward Kaluna's hand like an undulating snake. It had countless tiny feet moving in waves. Kaluna let out a whoop.

"You O.K.?" I called.

"Centipede! Da buggah is on me!"

I knew too well the centipede's painful and poisonous bite, which can send even a strong man like Kaluna to the hospital.

When I crouched down to check on the guide, the many-legged insect was weaving its way across the trail.

"Dat was one close one!" Kaluna shouted back through the *kiawe* boughs. "Da centipede ran ovah my hand, but he nevah sting."

"Come out of dere before you get hurt, bruddah."

"Jus' anoddah few feet to da kine–plastic bag or whatevah." He edged toward the elusive gleam. I heard him groan as he apparently stretched out his hand. "Got da bag!"

"Plastic bag?" I asked. "What's in it?"

"Hū!" Kaluna slid out from under the brush with a weathered Ziploc bag containing three spent syringes. Though mist and rain had fallen throughout this last month, inside that sealed bag the syringes remained dry as bone.

I dared to hope for usable fingerprints.

twenty-two

Kaluna and I continued down the trail to Kalaupapa and searched the village for more clues. Fruitlessly. Later we hiked back up with our only potential evidence: three spent syringes.

At the trailhead we stopped to quench our thirst and catch our breath. I told Kaluna I needed another favor.

"Now what I goin' ask may sound *lōlō*—crazy, you know—but I gotta ask." I peered into the mule guide's eyes.

"Jus' ask."

"We gotta exhume Coco."

"Do what fo' Coco?" His brow furrowed.

"Dig 'em up," I said. "You can get one backhoe from da Moloka'i Ranch, eh?"

"'*Ae*. But goin' take a while fo' put da backhoe on da trailer and haul 'em hea."

"How long?"

"Two, t'ree hours."

"Den how long fo' dig up da grave?"

"T'irty minutes," he said. "Counting da shovel work, too. But no mattah." He grinned. "I put 'em in hea', I can dig 'em out."

"Jus' one more t'ing. You got one veterinarian?"

Kaluna nodded. "Dr. Wyllie."

"Call Dr. Wyllie." I checked my watch. "Almost noon now. Ask 'em if he like come hea' at . . ."

"Not *he,*" Kaluna interrupted. "Dr. Wyllie one *wahine.*"

"O.K.—ask her if she can come at t'ree."

"What reason I goin' give?"

"Blood test fo' Coco." With my forefinger I made a needle-like gesture poking his arm. "We gonna send da blood to one mainland lab fo' drug check."

Kaluna dashed up the winding red road to the phone in the mule stable. I followed, then hopped into my rented car and raced back to Kaunakakai.

Drugs and drug paraphernalia pointed first to the doctor, obviously. But while Benjamin Goto had the means, he seemed to have less motive than the other suspects. This, coupled with the fact that just about anyone can possess syringes and illegal drugs, kept my attention focused on the others.

Did Milton Yu trade in harder drugs than *pakalōlō?* Did Heather Linborg dabble in dope? Did the wealthy Parke partake with her? And might Emery Archibald's proclivity for drugs be revealed through the identity of his secret companion? Trying to picture the stiff Rush McWhorter shooting up strained my imagination, but he might well have worked behind the scenes. No matter, I would cast my net wide to catch the guilty—be it one or all.

I was still mentally casting that net when I pulled up to the Moloka'i Beach Hotel. I made a quick call to check on Adrienne—still no change—then approached the front desk. My request to see the housemaid Mele had suggested I interview was greeted with a scowl. The new receptionist on duty seemed to instantly dislike me.

"Raine will not see you," she said, hands defiantly on hips.

Was it my sweat-glazed face or my rank T-shirt and board shorts?

"There must be some mistake," I tried to explain. "You see, last night Mele said . . ."

The scowling lady interrupted. "Don't play games. I know who you are."

"I'm Kai Cooke." I handed her my card. "I've never met Raine."

She glanced at the card. "You're not baby Kanoe's father?"

"I'm a private detective."

She eyed me up and down. "You don't look like a private detective."

"I've just come from Kalaupapa. I'm working on a case that Raine could help solve. Now, would you please call her?"

"She's cleaning the beachfront cottages." The receptionist pointed. "Over there."

Among the dozen or so beachside cottages, I found one with the door opened to a housekeeping cart. I knocked, then walked in. An attractive local woman with raven hair was snugging a fitted sheet over a queen-sized bed.

"Raine?"

She glanced up warily. Her forehead shone with beads of perspiration.

"Mele suggested I talk with you about a case I'm working on." I gave her my card. "I'm a private detective."

Raine handed back the card without looking at it. "If Moku sent you about custody of Kanoe, you can forget it."

"I have no client named Moku," I assured her. "In fact, I rarely work on Molokaʻi. I'm only here to investigate the death of a Honolulu woman on the Kalaupapa cliffs."

"Oh, da mule accident?" Raine's expression changed, and so did her speech. "Why you nevah say so?"

"Maybe you like help me wit' da case?" I replied in kind, heartened at a possible breakthrough.

"Last night Mele wen' show me in da hotel registah da name Archibald. He wen' stay in one oceanfront cottage wit' anoddah man guy name Stevens. Dey come Septembah t'ird and stay t'rough da seventh. You can remembah dem?"

"Was more than one mont' ago," Raine said. "Plenny guest come since den."

"Maybe dese two guest particulah. Maybe call attention to demselves?" I tried to jog her memory.

"What dis Archibald look like?"

"Slender *haole*. 'Bout forty. He wear fancy kine glasses—tortoiseshell—and dress elegant. Pinstripe suit. Scarf. Dat kine stuffs."

"Hmmm . . ." Raine was thinking.

"Oh, almost forget. He wear one spicy masculine cologne."

"I t'ink I remembah da man you call Archibald."

"What you remembah?"

"I t'ink he and da oddah guy—dat Stevens—dey *māhū*."

"*Māhū?*" I wondered if she had the wrong pair. "Da two men gay?"

"Two *men?*" Raine raised her raven brows. "One was only boy."

"Stevens was one boy?"

"Nineteen, twenty, max. Big muscles, you know. Liked fo' show them off. And da tattoo of one knife on his arm. How I forget dat?"

Stephan's bloody dagger. Suddenly it came to me. Stevens was Archibald's young assistant. I recalled Archibald's nervousness around the boy in my presence.

"Archibald and da boy wen' take drugs?" I tried to make a connection to the three syringes.

"I dunno," Raine said. "I nevah see dat kine in da room."

"Dey act funny kine," I said, "like maybe under da influence?"

Raine shook her head. "Dat's all I can remembah."

"Thanks, eh? You've been a big help."

I wished I could have thanked Raine with cash—to help with her baby—but if she were deposed to testify, the first thing the defense attorney would ask was if she had been given anything in exchange for her testimony. A potentially valuable witness might be erased. I could over-tip a bartender with impunity, but slipping a few bills to a chamber maid in a hotel where I was not a guest was another matter.

I said goodbye to Raine, wondering why Archibald's young friend hadn't taken the mule tour that day. Upon reflection, the answer seemed clear. For his business' sake, Archibald probably wouldn't want to have been seen with the boy.

Driving back toward Kalaupapa, I tried to sort things out. Archibald had come to Moloka'i, at least in part, to enjoy his muscular young assistant. So what did it mean? Was Archibald merely a middle-aged family man who sought an exotic getaway with his paramour? Or was he, and perhaps Stephan, connected to the *hui?* Since Archibald's travel business depended on Hawai'i tourism, he had some slim motive of his own to silence the woman bent on derailing Kalaupapa Cliffs. Maybe the *hui* had something on him, or he owed them a favor.

Archibald could not be ruled out. I stomped the accelerator and darted toward the cliffs of Kalaupapa.

twenty-three

When I returned to the trailhead, Kaluna had already dug a big hole. He sat up high at the controls of a dull orange backhoe, its long, thundering claw tearing away at the grave. Red earth surrounded the deepening pit.

Next to the grave stood a wispy woman with delicate features and angel-fine hair. She was young—fresh from veterinary school, I imagined—and looked more like a violinist than a large-animal vet.

When Kaluna saw me, he shut off the earthmoving machine and climbed down. I introduced myself to Dr. Wyllie, who extended her doll-sized hand, saying "Hello" in a surprisingly strong voice. Kaluna carried his shovel to the open grave and began spading gingerly around the edges.

"Mr. Cooke, you would like blood drawn from the dead mule?" she asked.

I nodded. "I'll be sending the blood to a California lab for analysis."

"And how long has the animal been buried?"

"One mont'," Kaluna said from Coco's grave, pitching out a shovel of red earth.

Dr. Wyllie frowned. "In this hot, humid weather, the mule may be decomposing by now. I'll be lucky to find a single vein."

"We need a blood sample to prove the mule was drugged." I showed her the three syringes in the sealed plastic bag.

"These are 3-cc syringes," she explained, "used more often on humans than large animals."

"Whoever did this probably wasn't a vet."

Dr. Wyllie's frown deepened. "I'll see what I can do." The slight doctor walked toward the backhoe, its orange claw now resting on mounds of red earth surrounding the open grave.

Down in the pit with the dead mule, Kaluna tossed up one last shovel of damp soil. Hands covering his nose from the stench, the *paniolo's* eyes were watering.

"Dat's Coco," he choked out. "But not like I bury him."

Kaluna had cleared off enough red dirt so that we could see what was left of the carcass. As he climbed out, I peered in. The stench was unbearable. All I could discern of the animal was a mere skeleton covered by a thin hide. His once-rounded haunches and broad girth of muscle and fat and fur were gone. If there were any blood in the veins of that carcass, if there were any veins at all, I would count it a miracle. Kaluna walked slowly to the precipice overlooking Kalaupapa. He gazed silently at the distant village.

Dr. Wyllie pulled an empty syringe from her bag, then donned a surgical mask and latex gloves. She climbed down into the grave and began searching for veins. I pulled out my camera and photographed her as she checked from rump to muzzle, then shook her head and climbed out again.

"No veins we can use." The pale doctor looked relieved as she pulled down her surgical mask and began to remove her latex gloves. "Maybe a week or two ago, but not now."

Without a blood sample showing Coco had been drugged, my case was fast slipping away. I tried to think.

"Wait!" I motioned to Dr. Wyllie to keep on her gloves. "Are the mule's vital organs intact—liver and kidney and all?"

"I can't say," she replied warily. "I'd have to surgically open the carcass." Dr. Wyllie flashed that sweet frown again.

"I'm just remembering a case," I explained. "A Kaua'i man found in a pineapple field—dead for more than a month. He yielded up a liver with enough blood to show evidence of drugs."

"Well, if you want to go to that extreme, blood in the liver stores drug residues at ten times the concentration of blood in the veins."

"Perfect." Now I was hopeful again. "All we need is the mule's liver."

Dr. Wyllie was now grimacing. She didn't seem to relish the assignment, but began removing surgical instruments from her medical bag—scalpels, clamps, some other stainless tools. She snapped her surgical mask back into place, snugged her latex gloves, and again climbed into the hole. I took more photos as she cut along Coco's gut, opening a gaping cavity under the ribs. When she lifted the severed hide, the stench that emerged was beyond foul. Despite the stink, I made myself move in closer to snap more photos.

In a little while the petite vet climbed from the grave with grime and gore from her fingertips to her elbows. That nasty death smell followed her. But she had delivered the trophy. In her hands was a liver the size of a football. It looked in amazingly good shape.

Dr. Wyllie said nothing. She seemed in a somber mood.

"Are you all right?" I asked.

She nodded and removed her gory gloves, her strong voice fading. "This was my first surgery on a dead mule."

"And I bet you hope it's your last."

She gestured to the grimy organ. "To send this liver to California, you'll need a Styrofoam mailer. And an ice pack wouldn't hurt . . ." She paused. "I've got a mailer in my van, but the ice pack you'll have to find elsewhere."

"I'll pick one up in Honolulu. I'm catching the next flight out."

I stepped to where Kaluna stood, still gazing down at the distant sea. Though in a hurry to take my prize back to Honolulu, I didn't rush the mule guide. For him, opening the grave had evidently opened old wounds.

I put my arm on Kaluna's shoulder. "Coco nevah make da *wahine,* Sara, go *hala,*" I said. "Was not his fault."

"*Mahalo,* Kai." He smiled slightly. "If you nevah come hea to *nīele,* to nose around, I always wonder 'bout Coco. Now I know. He stay one good mule."

Kaluna climbed onto the backhoe and began covering his mule with red earth, while Dr. Wyllie and I hiked up the winding dirt road to the stables. She placed the oversized liver into a plastic bag fetched from her van, then put the sealed bag in a Styrofoam mailer. Next to the liver, in another of the doctor's plastic bags, I set in one of the three syringes Kaluna had found on the trail.

I had the veterinarian handwrite a statement summarizing her procedures, which I took with me on my flight back to Honolulu. A few fellow passengers eyed curiously the box in my lap. Fortunately, the liver's unspeakable odor was trapped inside.

The Twin-Otter landed in Honolulu at four-thirty. I rushed to a drugstore to buy an ice pack, then back to the airport, barely beating FedEx's five o'clock deadline to fly my parcel overnight to San Francisco. I debated showering off the day's filth before visiting Adrienne. All things considered, it seemed unimportant. When I got to her hospital room, I found her as I had left her— pale, cool, and breathing slowly. I reassured both of us aloud that I was making progress toward vindicating her sister.

"We're going to win," I told her. "And you're going to wake up to share in the celebration."

Back at my Waikīkī apartment, two phone messages awaited: one from Niki, which, like her photo, I tried to ignore; the second was from Archibald, who now recalled that although all four mule riders had taken the Kalaupapa bus tour, the overweight physician, Dr. Goto, had asked to be dropped off early at the restroom near the tethered mules. The doctor had apparently apologized profusely, regretting that he had drunk too much water after the hot ride down.

The suspect with the least motive, Dr. Goto was, however, most likely to possess the means to sedate Coco—syringes and drugs. After dropping out of the bus tour, he could have slipped among the mules, eluded Kaluna, and injected Coco. But why?

Goto's complicity wasn't a scenario I had much envisioned. Regardless, I needed the doctor's fingerprints, and the sooner the better. If Goto's prints matched those on the three syringes, the case was nearly solved. Drug evidence linking the syringes to the mule's collapse would be the clincher. But I wasn't banking on the solution being this easy. Besides, maybe Archibald was attempting to shift suspicion from himself, if only to keep my nose out of his private life. Or maybe the paunchy Goto really had been dehydrated.

Later that night I crawled into bed with the evening *Star-Bulletin*. On the front page, a story secured one more piece of this complex puzzle—Baron Taniguchi's bloated body had been found floating in Honolulu Harbor. He had been shot, execution style, in the head.

twenty-four

Before sunrise Tuesday morning, I phoned the California lab that does my blood work. Though barely twilight in Honolulu, the laboratory technicians at Bio-Tech in Daly City had already taken their mid-morning coffee break.

The lab manager, Ernie, confirmed that the Styrofoam mailer had arrived that morning by FedEx. Elaborating on my transmittal letter, I explained that the enclosed syringe probably contained traces of the suspected drug. I suggested a sedative such as morphine.

What I needed, I added, was the drug identified in both the blood and the syringe. The job was rush. Even though blood samples sent from Hawai'i normally took a week or more to analyze, I needed results in two days.

The manager laughed. "You've got to be kidding, Kai. We have a two-week backlog. Besides, the comprehensive drug screen takes several days—even if we didn't have a backlog."

"Just test for morphine. It's a strong hunch I have."

"Then you want only the presumptive opiate test?"

"Yes—and fast."

"With luck we might complete that test in two days, if we had no backlog."

"I'll call you Wednesday afternoon for the results."

"You can call whenever you like, Kai." He laughed again. "But that doesn't guarantee . . ."

"Ernie, this is life or death."

"We've got a half dozen jobs like that!"

I took a long, deep breath. "I'm in big trouble, Ernie. You've got to help me out."

He was silent for a moment. "I'll see what I can do."

I hung up the phone. The Land Zoning Board's charade hearing to approve the Chancellor Trust resort was only three days away. By Thursday, at the latest, I needed to present my case against the *hui* to the FBI. Then a federal judge might suspend the hearing pending an investigation—that is, if I got the crucial blood evidence by Thursday. Without it, neither the FBI nor a federal judge was likely to buy a loony story about murder by mule drugging.

As the rising sun peeked above the misty Ko'olau Mountains and flooded my *lānai,* I dialed the office of Dr. Benjamin Goto. He wasn't in at this early hour, so I left a message:

"Dr. Goto, could you see me briefly today? I'd appreciate your help in identifying a suspect in the Sara Ridgely-Parke case. Please leave a message at my office as to your best time. *Mahalo.*"

Whether or not the doctor responded, I wanted to be ready for him. With a fingerprint kit I keep in my flat I dusted the two remaining syringes. The Ziploc bag containing them, as I had hoped, also preserved several prints. Using pressure-wound tape, I pulled each print off the syringes and fixed it on a three-by-five card. This resulted in six cards containing reasonably good prints–whether Goto's or one of the other suspects. Perhaps by this afternoon I would know.

Before leaving for the hospital to visit Adrienne, I grabbed Niki's photo from my nightstand. I removed Sara's speech from where it was still sandwiched between the snapshot and its cardboard backing. Then with glass cleaner and paper towels, I sprayed and polished the framed photo until it shone like mirror. I slipped Niki's gleaming snapshot in a paper bag and placed the bag, along with my fingerprint kit, the syringes, and Sara's speech, in my briefcase.

By eight that morning, I was heading for the Halekōkua Medical Center. Cruising along the Ala Wai Canal, I glimpsed the smoke grey van in my rearview mirror. Trying to lose it seemed pointless, since the *hui* most likely knew where I was going. I turned right onto the McCully Street bridge, crossed the canal, then steered my Impala *mauka* toward the hospital on Punahou Street. When my destination became clear, the van dropped back and turned off on a side street.

I detoured to a one-hour photo shop at King and University streets, and dropped off the pictures I had snapped on Moloka'i of Kaluna discovering the three syringes and Dr. Wyllie extracting Coco's liver. Along with the veterinarian's written statement, these photos would document the real cause of Sara's death. All that was left for me to do was uncover its agents.

At the hospital, Adrienne slept pale and quiet in her room—an oxygen tube still assisting her breathing and an IV dripping fluids into her arm. When I touched her hand, her skin was neither cold nor warm. She seemed precariously balanced between death and life.

I left her connected to this world through only a few tubes and that gritty, determined spirit of hers that had gotten me into this.

Driving back to Maunakea Street, I kept a close eye on my rearview mirror. No van. Its absence seemed almost more ominous than if the *hui* had kept right on my tail.

Along the way I picked up my Moloka'i photos. Clear. Unmistakable. Kaluna's slithering under *kiawe* bushes to fetch the Ziploc bag and Dr. Wyllie's removal of Coco's liver were frozen in time. I could still smell the stench from that grave.

Business was slow this Tuesday morning at Fujiyama's. Just one customer picked over strands of orchids in the refrigerated display cases. In the back, Chastity and Joon were stringing *pīkake* blooms. Such a fresh fragrance arose from that *pīkake* that I asked the *lei* girls to string three intertwined strands for Adrienne. One strand of *pīkake* traditionally represents friendship; three strands, the highest degree.

I climbed the stairs to my office and listened to my phone messages:

"Eh, brah, how much you charge fo' find one missing surfboard? One dumb dodo steal mine at Hale'iwa . . ."

One drawback of calling myself the "Surfing Detective." The next message made me more alert.

"This is Dr. Goto's office," said a crisp, businesslike receptionist. "The doctor can see you this afternoon at five o'clock."

Goto had taken the bait. Though I was a little surprised at the late hour of the appointment. Since he saw patients only from ten to two, I wondered why he was waiting until five.

I picked up my briefcase and locked my office behind me. Passing back through Mrs. Fujiyama's, I grabbed Adrienne's *lei*, and paced down Maunakea toward my bank, First Oʻahu Savings on King Street, where a clerk ushered me into a private booth and retrieved my safe deposit box. From my briefcase I pulled each piece of evidence I had collected and put it into the safety box, retaining copies of the fingerprints I had dusted from the syringes.

It was nearly ten-thirty when I returned to my parking garage. With six hours until the interview with Dr. Goto, I did something not every detective would understand. I drove to the North Shore and went surfing.

At exactly five o'clock I was riding a mirrored elevator to the eighteenth floor of Goto's office building. The empty waiting room looked the same as before. But today, no one sat behind the desk.

Within moments of my arrival, the doctor himself emerged from his inner office. His pale skin, hanging jowls, and rounded belly did lend credibility to Archibald's report that Goto had to drop out of the Kalaupapa bus tour to relieve himself.

"Please come into my office, Mr. Cooke." Goto greeted me with his smiling almond eyes. "It's a pleasure to see you again." His cordiality, however, failed to conceal a hint of nervousness.

As Goto slipped behind his teak desk, I noticed the photo from Caesar's Palace was gone from his wall.

"Sorry about the short notice," I said, starting my spiel. "I'm grateful for your help in solving this case."

"Anything I can do," he said graciously. "My receptionist told me you wish to speak again about the unfortunate accident on Molokaʻi."

"That's correct." I opened my briefcase, pulling out the paper bag containing the framed photo of Niki. I turned the picture toward him.

"That's an attractive young woman," Goto said, staring at Niki's string bikini and sexy smile.

"I'm hoping you can identify her."

He leaned forward, studying her face. "She doesn't look like the criminal type."

"Oh, you'd be surprised, doctor, what innocent-looking people can do." I handed him the photo. "Here, take a closer look."

Goto seemed to be trembling as he grabbed hold of the clean glass.

"Did you see this woman on Moloka'i on the day of Sara Ridgely-Parke's death?"

"She looks vaguely familiar."

"Go ahead. Take your time."

The doctor squinted at Niki's smiling face. "It's funny," he finally said. "I fly quite often to medical conferences on the mainland. Denver. Chicago. Indianapolis. This woman looks like a flight attendant I've seen on several trips."

"That so?" I cringed. I hadn't thought Goto would actually recognize Niki. "You also fly to Las Vegas, don't you?" I tried to change the subject.

Dr. Goto frowned. "Not anymore." His guard, which had been perceptibly relaxing as my questions focused away from him, now went back up.

"Sorry I can't do any better with your suspect." He handed back the photo.

"Thanks for trying." I slipped it back into the paper bag, then tucked the bag in my brief case.

Dr. Goto rose, signaling that the interview had ended.

"May I ask just one more question before I leave?"

"Surely." He seemed to brace himself slightly.

"It was reported that you did not complete the Kalaupapa bus tour—that you were dropped off early to use the restroom. Is that correct?"

"I'm embarrassed to say, yes." Goto smiled self-consciously. "I was quite dehydrated after the long, hot mule ride and I drank a large quantity of water to compensate."

"How did you occupy yourself while the others completed the tour?"

"I sat down and rested, of course."

"Near the mules?" I studied his face.

He winked playfully. "I stayed upwind of the mules, if you know what I mean."

"Thank you, Doctor." I headed for the door.

"My pleasure." He made a little bow.

I saw myself out with Niki's photo, covered with Goto's prints, tucked safely in my briefcase. My hunch was that the doctor was attempting a mediocre acting job. Now with his prints all over my frame, I would finally know for sure.

In the parking lot below Goto's mirrored tower, I unlocked my Impala and set the briefcase next to Adrienne's *pīkake lei* on the front seat. I was so elated about getting the doctor's fingerprints, I didn't see the smoke grey van pull up behind me.

twenty-five

Three big mokes—huge, meaty local boys—yanked me from my Impala and tossed me into the van. Before I had stopped rolling around in the back, we were speeding down Ala Moana Boulevard toward Waikīkī.

One of the big men sat in back with me, where there were no seats, blocking the van's sliding door. He must have tipped the scales at three hundred, easy. None of the mokes spoke to me. I said nothing to them. A warm, salty-tasting liquid dripped down my face. *Blood.* I must have cut my forehead.

As the van slowed in traffic along Waikīkī Beach—where camera-toting tourists awaited another perfect sunset—then curved around Diamond Head and its lavish seaside estates, I began to doubt my hunches on this case. J. Gregory Parke I had least suspected. But now that we were headed for Kāhala—his ritzy neighborhood—I wondered. Could Parke be behind all this? And was it an ominous sign that none of my abductors took the slightest precaution to conceal our route from me?

Suddenly the van turned off Diamond Head Road short of Parke's colonial castle, headed *makai* down a palm-lined private lane, then pulled up to an imposing black wrought-iron gate with a dozen spikes shaped like the ace of spades. The gate opened automatically and the van glided over flagstones onto the grounds of a magnificent oceanfront estate.

My captors unloaded me, still without saying a word. The only sounds were the clacking of coconut palm fronds along the secluded beach and the constant splash of waves.

The mansion looked Mediterranean, with bright white walls and red tile roof that might have pleased my eyes under other circumstances. Surrounding us were expansive tropical gardens, black granite pool and spa, and clay tennis courts encircled by those whispering palms. A four-car carriage house, with only one door open, revealed a flame red Lamborghini. The exotic Italian machine displayed a personalized plate: "Manny."

Manny Lee, my cousin Alika's famous uncle, had not laid eyes on me since I was a little *keiki*. I faintly recalled him singing *"Aloha 'Oe,"* that familiar Hawaiian song of farewell, at my parents' funeral. Halfway through, his voice broke. The international star—and local tough guy—overcome by emotion.

I was taken to a marble *lānai* overlooking the sea, where he reclined on a chaise lounge, nursing a high ball. Manny was fifty-ish. His long hair black, but turning salt-and-pepper. Pixie-like face of Hawaiian and Chinese aspect, youthful considering the life it had seen. Gold chain around his neck and gold Hawaiian bracelet on one wrist emblazoned with his name.

Manny said to the biggest of the three mokes, "Bobo, t'anks, eh?"

As the trio walked away, my suspicions about the singer were instantly confirmed.

Manny Lee was a legend in and out of the islands. He was the most famous living Hawaiian pop singer, owner of multiple gold records. Tales of his exploits with women, with money, and with drink and drugs were legion. His association with underworld thugs made him feared. Messing with Manny—so it was said—led to broken bones. Of late, he had supposedly turned over the proverbial new leaf and become a leading investor in local enterprises.

He gestured to the *lānai* chair across from him. I sat. The setting sun glinted blindingly on three gold records visible in a nearby cabana and also starkly illuminated Manny's face. In the fiery orange glow he looked both saintly and devilish, a wayward spirit poised between the poles of goodness and evil. I gazed warily at this pop luminary, this aging star, this distant relation through marriage who had summoned me.

"Long time no see, Kai," said Manny in his melodious tones.

"Back when Mom and Dad died."

"I sang at their funeral," Manny recalled. "You just one *keiki* then, maybe too young to remembah."

"I remembah." I daubed a blood drop trickling down my forehead.

"Kai, family—*'ohana*—is important. You marry yet?"

I shook my head.

"Find one nice local girl. Raise some *keiki*. Living alone no good. I know." He winked.

"Thanks for the advice."

"One more piece of advice." Manny glanced toward his glinting gold disks, his eyes scouring the cabana as if searching for someone. "Kai, let da *wahine* who wen' fall from da mule on Moloka'i rest in peace."

I studied his illuminated face. "Stop my investigation?"

Manny again glanced away. "If you not one family membah, you awready be dead."

"Are you in the *hui?* With Zia and the rest?"

"Kai, I cannot make gold records forevah." He shrugged in a gesture of resignation, or maybe apology? "All entertainahs do business on da side. You be loyal and someday da *hui* cut you in, too."

I sat motionless, not wanting to believe what I was hearing.

"Take one vacation for a few days. My travel agent already book you in one oceanfront suite in Kona. First class. Meals and everyt'ing on me. Bobo give you da tickets when you leave."

"Go to Kona? What for?"

Manny peered into my eyes. "You stay in Kona until aftah Friday's zoning board hearing. You get 'um, Kai?"

"Yeah, I get 'um." At that moment I understood better than he could imagine—the arrogance of power that believes itself above the law.

"Your *'ohana* no like you die young, Kai. I doing this for dem. We all family and grow up close."

The three mokes trudged slowly into view like foraging bears. Manny rose and shook my hand. As the trio led me away in the dying sunset, Manny called in our direction.

"Kai, no forget. *'Ohana!*"

When I looked back, Manny was no longer alone. Another man, thin as a ghost and barely five feet tall in a white suit and aviator sunglasses, had emerged from the cabana and was whispering in his ear. They stood together in conspiratorial closeness, as the newcomer puffed on a brown cigarette whose raw, pungent odor I could smell from twenty feet away. Then it dawned on me: The other man was Umbro Zia.

Manny nodded to Zia in a gesture of reassurance as the two conversed in whispers. I assumed the nodding pertained to me. The *hui* had me, Manny was probably explaining to Zia. I would no longer interfere.

The mokes loaded me back into the grey van, more gently this time. The hefty driver, Bobo, handed me a packet stuffed with a first-class airline ticket, hotel voucher, and a wad of crisp green bills. Ben Franklins. Hundreds. Also inside on a handwritten slip was a Big Island phone number and a name, "Lani." Beneath that, in Manny's own hand: "Call Lani. She one *'ono* babe and she show you a good time."

I sat on the floor of the van next to a computer, monitor, and keyboard that hadn't been there before. The equipment resembled my stolen PC. As the van screeched up the flagstone driveway toward the automatic gate, I looked at the computer more closely. It *was* my PC.

The ride back to Goto's mirrored tower was uneventful. In the quiet, gathering darkness I contemplated the significance of my trip. Whatever Goto's role in the murder, whatever tangled relationships existed between Sara and Parke and McWhorter, there was no longer any doubt that the *hui* was at the center of it all.

The van pulled up to my car in the flood-lighted parking lot. As I climbed out, one of the mokes lifted the PC from the van and put it on the pavement. Before I could open my trunk, the van was gone.

My briefcase still sat miraculously on the front seat. I clicked the locks open. There was the bag with Niki's framed photo in it. The *hui* must have felt Manny's warning would be sufficient to send me packing to Kona. I loaded my computer into the trunk and drove to the hospital in a heady cloud of perfume from the *pīkake lei* I'd bought that morning for Adrienne.

By the time I reached her bedside that evening most visitors had already departed. Her stillness intensified the quiet.

Drawing close to her, I explained that I knew now who had killed her sister. And I would be back soon, I said in farewell, to tell her how the rest of the business turned out. I kissed her unresponsive cheek, the same cool, pale white as the *pīkake* blossoms I placed in her open hand.

Before leaving the hospital, I called the Honolulu office of the FBI, closed for the night. I left a voice-mail message for an agent I knew named Javier. Not certain who might be listening in, I was deliberately vague:

"Bill, expect a fax from a mainland lab. I'll explain later."

Back at Mrs. Fujiyama's flower shop, I lugged my computer past the darkened display windows, around to the side door, and up the fire stairs to my office. Connecting the PC to its power and printer cables, I switched it on. All documents relating to the Ridgely-Parke case had been erased, while every other document remained. Neat job.

I shut down the computer, then turned to Niki's photo. If she only knew how much she was helping on this case. I dusted the glass and frame for fingerprints. There were several good ones. I checked them against the six cards containing prints from the syringes. They matched.

twenty-six

Until the sable hour of three the next morning, I mulled over the two options Manny had laid before me: Take an all-expenses-paid trip to Kona or get myself drilled.

I no longer doubted that the *hui* could do whatever it wanted with me. To stay on Oʻahu was tantamount to suicide. Besides, I couldn't save the cliffs of Kalaupapa if I were dead.

That decided it. At 10:45 a.m. I would board the plane to Kona. *Holoholo, brah. Time fo' one pleasure trip.*

I packed a small duffel with just enough clothes for an overnight. Into my briefcase I put a microcassette tape recorder, then the cards containing Goto's fingerprints and Niki's photo covered with more of his prints. In a side pocket of the briefcase I slipped the airline tickets, hotel voucher, and Manny's cash. I also tucked in my Smith & Wesson. Something told me I might need it in the next forty-eight hours.

At seven I phoned Bio-Tech Labs. No results yet, but Ernie hoped to have a preliminary analysis by four in the afternoon, California time.

"Even if you don't hear from me again," I told him, "fax a copy of the blood work to Agent Javier, Honolulu office of the FBI."

By eight, I was heading for the Halekōkua Medical Center. Within two blocks the smoke grey van appeared behind me. Bobo and his pals must want to make sure I get to the airport on time. *How thoughtful.* They tailed me to the hospital, then pulled to the curb on Punahou Street when I turned into the garage.

I rode the elevator up to Adrienne's floor, passing the nurses' station as I walked down the hall to her room.

"Oh, Mr. Cooke!" said an animated nurse. "Good news. Ms. Ridgely opened her eyes this morning."

"Opened her eyes?" I was stoked.

"She hasn't spoken yet," the nurse said. "But Dr. Majerian is hopeful."

"Thank you." I rushed into Adrienne's room. Her eyes were closed again. She lay silent and motionless as she had for nearly a week, oxygen flowing to her through her tube. But where before her cheeks had been pale, now they showed hints of color. Her chestnut hair, too, seemed to have regained some of its luster. And her long, slender fingers curled around the *pīkake lei* I had brought last night, the fragrant white blossoms still breathing their perfume.

I sat with Adrienne for a half hour, wishing she would open her eyes—for her sake as well as mine. But that didn't happen.

Before leaving I clutched her hand, softer and warmer than before. Then a troubling thought occurred to me: What if Adrienne awoke and started talking about Kalaupapa Cliffs before Friday's hearing? How might the *hui* respond? They were watching her no doubt as closely as I was.

On my way out I explained to the on-duty nurse that for Adrienne's safety, we would need to order twenty-four hour protection–immediately. I called Island-Wide Security, who reassured me with military crispness that the first guard would arrive at the hospital within minutes.

I waited in the parking lot until the security car drove up, then pulled away from the hospital, aiming for the Mānoa Valley campus of the University of Hawai'i. The smoke grey van caught up with me after a block and tailgated me all the way there.

School was in session. Students on mopeds and in lowered Hondas that buzzed like angry bees swarmed the streets. I pulled into the law school parking lot. The van crawled by and found a nearby parking space.

From my briefcase I removed the microcassette recorder, set it to "voice activated," and slipped it into my shirt pocket. Ready, I stepped into the bunker-like complex of the law school and walked the narrow hallway to McWhorter's office, knocked, and waited. When his door finally swung open, he looked surprised. A Marlboro Light dangled from his lip.

"Well, the 'Surfing Detective.'" He stood up straight, puffing on his smoke. "To what do I owe . . ."

"So you remember me?"

"How could I forget?" He exhaled a hazy plume. "That surfer gimmick actually works."

McWhorter gestured to a chair, then slid behind his desk, silk aloha shirt framed by a leather throne. He puffed again and ran long fingers over his close-cropped hair.

"You know about Adrienne." I stated more than asked as my microcassette recorded our words.

"Terrible accident," McWhorter said in his high, thin monotone. "Can you imagine someone hitting her and just driving away?"

"It wasn't an accident," I eyed him. "No more than Sara's death was an accident. Or your student, Baron Taniguchi's."

"I wouldn't know," McWhorter coolly replied.

"No need to play games anymore. The *hui* has bought me off, too. They're sending me to Kona—all expenses paid—until after Friday's hearing on Kalaupapa Cliffs."

"Then you're easily bought off, Mr. Surfing Detective."

"What choice did I have? They would have dumped me in the harbor like Baron Taniguchi."

"I thought surfers were bold and brave."

"Surfers *are* brave, but not crazy—at least not this one. Anyway, you're the key figure in all this, not me."

He dragged on his Marlboro Light, his face as fixed as a plaster mask.

"The *hui* could never have gotten Sara or Baron Taniguchi without you. You hacked into Sara's computer and intercepted her email. That's how you discovered her Moloka'i itinerary and Baron's fishing trip to Bamboo Ridge."

McWhorter rocked back and blew more smoke. "They should have known better than to send confidential messages by email."

"You conveyed those messages straight to the Chancellor Trust." I tried to get him to echo or at least elaborate on my incriminations.

"I'm the trust's legal counsel," McWhorter said, not biting. "Had I found such vital documents—and I'm not saying I did—I couldn't very well withhold them."

"You did find some vital documents." I tried to keep him talking. "But you missed one—a crucial one."

Tiny cracks appeared in his plaster. I'd hit a nerve.

"I didn't say I found anything," McWhorter repeated. "If I had considered violating the law by going through Sara's records, it would have been merely to save her reputation. She had a private life you wouldn't imagine."

"Wasn't it your own reputation you were trying to save? Sara rejected you. She turned you away. That's why you had to get even after she married Parke. That's why you tipped off the *hui* about her trip to Moloka'i."

"Pure fiction."

"Then why did Dr. Goto just yesterday accuse you of orchestrating Sara's murder?" I had to make something up to widen those cracks in his plaster mask.

McWhorter snuffed his cigarette in the ashtray, then lit another. "It's no secret that 'quack' Goto owes the *hui* big time for his Vegas gambling debts. He would say anything to dig himself out."

"So Goto killed Sara to pay off gambling debts?"

"You can draw you own conclusions."

I looked at my watch. Nine thirty. "Maybe we can continue this conversation later. I've got a plane to catch."

I walked from his smoky office into the fresher air of the hall. While his cleverly worded responses probably wouldn't hold up as evidence against him, he had certainly provided a motive for Goto's role in Sara's murder.

twenty-seven

Keeping an eye on the van in my rearview mirror, I headed toward my bank on King Street as I replayed the taped conversation with McWhorter. His high voice came through as clearly as if he were sitting next to me. Satisfied, I popped out the cassette and deposited it in my bank box along with the other pieces of evidence.

By the time I turned back onto Nimitz Highway, both hands of the Aloha Tower clock were pointing to ten. I would just make my 10:45 flight to Kona.

I took the airport ramp, Bobo and his friends close behind. They parked a few spaces from my car in the inter-island garage, then followed me on foot to the elevator. At least they let me ride up to the terminal alone, but while checking in for my flight, I saw them lurking behind me again. *Are they going with me to Kona?*

As the ticket agent checked me in, I slipped an inter-island flight schedule into my briefcase.

"When is the last flight tonight from Hilo to Maui?" I asked in nearly a whisper.

The agent checked her computer monitor. "10:25 p.m., sir. Would you like me to hold you a seat?"

"No, thanks." I didn't want my name to appear on any reservation list. I took my ticket and briefcase, then walked toward the restrooms. The mokes split off from the passenger line without going through check-in.

Inside the men's restroom, a quick check revealed that I was alone except for one man in a toilet stall. Near the washbasins, a stainless steel trash receptacle—recently emptied by a custodian—stood against the tiled wall. It was the typical arrangement: a plastic liner set inside the stainless container. I lifted the nearly empty liner and pulled it out. At the bottom of the container lay a dozen extra liners, folded in neat little squares and stacked one upon the other. Opening my briefcase, I removed the Smith & Wesson and wrapped it in one of the liners, then placed the heavy package at the bottom of the neat stack.

My bet was that this trash bin wouldn't be emptied again for a while, and if it was, the gun probably wouldn't be noticed. I'd be returning for it soon anyway.

At 10:40, with the three mokes looking on, I ambled down the jetway onto a Boeing 737 bound for Kona. As Manny Lee had promised, my seat was in first class—a wide leather easy chair. I declined the complimentary cocktail, opting instead for guava punch. With less than forty-eight hours until the Kalaupapa Cliffs hearing, I needed a clear head.

Under the morning sun, the lush, surf-washed islands of Moloka'i, Lāna'i, and Maui shone like emeralds against the sapphire sea. The approach to Kona, by contrast, revealed a black wasteland of charred lava, the runway a thin white line etched in surrounding darkness. Though I had landed at Kona many times before, on this trip the black landscape looked especially foreboding.

The Boeing touched down smooth as silk. Inside the terminal a man in a chauffeur's uniform held an official-looking sign: Royal Kona Resort—Mr. Kai Cooke. The chauffeur retrieved my duffel from the luggage cart and escorted me to a black town car limo whose license plates said "Royal K." I climbed in.

The Royal Kona Resort was draped in coral pink bougainvillea and overlooked Keauhou Bay and its tide pools, which contained petroglyphs carved by ancient Hawaiians. Strolling the hotel's open-air lobby, I kept an eye out for signs of the *hui*. *Would Manny leave me alone in Kona? Doubtful.*

Once the bellboy ushered me into my suite, it was clear that Manny had forked out quite a sum for this little "vacation." My oceanfront room fronted the historic tide pools and rumbling surf. The view, as the tour books say, was breathtaking. Too bad I couldn't stick around and enjoy it.

Less than a minute after the bellboy had pocketed his tip—a five from Manny's stash—the phone rang.

"Kai," said the melodious voice, "you like da suite?"

"Manny, you really shouldn't have."

"Call Lani yet?"

"I just walked in the door."

"Lani's *'ono*." Manny sounded like he knew firsthand just how delicious she was.

"I'll give her a call."

"Once you see Lani, brah, you nevah want to leave Kona—*nevah!*" There was a pause. "Remembah, Kai . . ." Manny suddenly turned serious. "You're your Mamma's *keiki*."

I groped for an appropriate reply. Too late. *Click.* He was gone.

I sat on my *lānai* for more than an hour watching the surf spray the tide pools and wondering how to get aboard tonight's last flight from Hilo to Maui. Once I landed on Maui, I could sack out at the airport and catch the first flight on Thursday morning to Honolulu. Making it to the Hilo airport tonight was the problem. The *hui* would be watching. And if they caught me escaping from Kona, I doubted if even Manny himself could spare my life.

Later that afternoon while walking the grounds of the resort, I kept glancing behind me. Nobody. The *hui* was playing cagey. I wandered past tennis courts, a curving *koa* bar, then the narrow ribbon of black sand between tide pools. Still seeing no one, I doubled back to a pay phone by the bar and placed a call.

"Bio-Tech Labs," said a harried-sounding receptionist.

"Kai Cooke calling for Ernie DiBello."

"One moment . . ."

I checked my watch. It was nearly two in Hawai'i. That meant almost five in California. This would be my last chance today to get results from the blood analysis on Kaluna's mule. Since tomorrow, Thursday, I needed to turn over this crucial piece of evidence to the FBI, time was running out.

"Hello, Kai," Ernie answered. "The final report isn't ready yet, but preliminary results on the mule's liver indicate Demerol."

"Demerol?"

"It's a synthetic morphine commonly used as a sedative in humans, but seldom in such high concentrations."

"What did you find in the syringe?"

"Same thing–Demerol."

"You're the best, Ernie. I owe you a Mai Tai on Waikīkī Beach."

"I'm going to show up in paradise someday, Kai, to take you up on that offer," Ernie said, laughing.

"Fax that report to the FBI by tomorrow morning and I'll throw in a dinner, too."

"The Feds will have it tomorrow." Ernie hung up.

Returning to my room I noticed someone watching me. The man stood in the shadow of a planter ablaze with red ginger. He wasn't a big local guy like Manny's three mokes. He was *haole,* pale and thin. He could have been merely a mainland visitor, but the way he watched me suggested otherwise. When I glanced back from the elevator lobby, the man was gone.

Back in my suite I picked up the phone and dialed the number Manny had given me.

"Aloha . . ." answered a breathy voice.

"Lani?"

"Who's calling?" she asked playfully, as if she already knew.

"Kai Cooke. Manny Lee suggested I call you."

"Can't wait to meet you, Kai!" She sounded almost sincere. "Manny told me all about you."

"He's told me a lot about you, too. How about dinner tonight?"

"No need to ask. I'll pick you up at quarter to six. Everything's been arranged."

"Everything?"

"Well, just the dinner." Lani giggled. "What happens afterward is up to you."

twenty-eight

With three hours until Lani arrived, I swam and sunned at the resort's beach. My shadow stayed hidden at first. Then, reclining in a lounge chair behind the *Hawai'i Tribune Herald,* the thin man briefly exposed his pale face. He didn't look like he was having much fun.

When I left the beach at five, the man followed me. I stopped in at the ABC Store off the hotel's lobby, bought a woman's sun hat, and carried it away in a shopping bag. The thin man watched me from outside the store, then followed me to the elevators.

Up in my room I showered and dressed for dinner in front of the TV. The local news carried a slanted report on the Kalaupapa Cliffs project. Two supposed Moloka'i residents spoke in favor of the resort, both too slick to be believed.

The reporter mentioned Friday's Land Zoning Board hearing as the last step to approval of the development, as if approval were a foregone conclusion. No one from the coalition had been interviewed, nor was the coalition survey mentioned that showed 94 percent of Moloka'i's residents opposed the project. And, of course, no death toll was given.

At twenty minutes to six I rode the elevator to the lobby and stood outside by the valets waiting for Lani. The setting sun backlighted the tide pools in a butterscotch glow. A few minutes later she pulled up in a silver Porsche, waving through the sunroof. She screeched to the curb.

Slipping into the leather bucket on the passenger side, its soft hides reeking of newness, I offered her my hand. Lani warmed mine with both of hers and looked me square in the eyes.

"Manny didn't tell me you were so young."

"I'm thirty-four," I said, inhaling her heavy floral perfume. "I must have ten years on you."

Lani giggled. "I'll show you a good time."

She gunned the Porsche and we launched from the Royal Kona Hotel like a rocket. Suddenly I noticed on the dash the ominous word *turbo*.

"'*Ono*," Manny had called her. I could see why. Luminous eyes, jet black hair, slender tanned limbs. She looked wholesome, almost innocent. Her sweet perfume magnified this impression. But the plunging neckline of her black cocktail dress and her heavy eye shadow undercut it.

Lani ripped along the waterfront toward Kona around curves at a pace that would have flipped an ordinary car. She reeved that turbocharged 911 through its countless gears.

"I *love* to go fast," she said. "But I'm just learning to drive the Porsche . . ."

No truer words could have been spoken. I braced myself around each curve as Lani talked nonstop. She must have had a drink or two before picking me up. In a short span I learned that she had met Manny once when he performed in Kona. They hit it off. Soon she found herself on the singer's payroll, "entertaining" him and his guests when they visited the Big Island. It was a strange story. And a sad story. Though Lani probably didn't think so.

On one hair-raising turn, I popped opened the Porsche's glove box. Inside were two CDs, an Almond Joy candy bar, some loose condoms, and a Big Island map. I closed it back up and glanced behind us. Nobody. Was the thin man already at the restaurant? Or did he trust Manny's girl to chaperone me?

Lani pulled up to the Windjammer, a trendy Kona seafood spot along Ali'i Drive that resembled a yacht pointed into the breakers. She emerged from her car with a large black sequined handbag that matched her cocktail dress. She was a tall, statuesque woman—quite tall for a local girl—within a few inches of my own height.

Winding our way through the bustling restaurant—appointed with the spars and beams and fixtures of a seagoing galley—we emerged onto the bow deck overlooking the twilight surf. Lani ordered a Mai Tai and I, a beer. Our drinks arrived as we scanned the long menu. I also continued to scan the restaurant for the thin man. No sign of him.

Lani wasted no time putting away her Mai Tai. When the waiter arrived, she asked for another. We ordered dinner and a bottle of Chardonnay, then chatted as Lani slugged down her second drink. She was already getting a little woozy.

By the time our entrees came Lani was well into the wine. Her cheeks blushed like ripe mangos.

"Kai . . ." Lani smiled coyly and gripped my hand. "I . . . li-like yooo."

The more she drank, the more she slurred. Despite her undeniable allure, I felt sorry for Lani. She had gotten caught in Manny Lee's web. A new Porsche, some cash, and no doubt a condo by the sea had been her payment. I wondered if ten years down the road Lani might concede she had made a mistake. Her heavy drinking made me suspect that already she had an inkling.

By the time we finished dessert, Lani was in no shape to drive. I paid the check with one of Manny's hundreds, then eased her limp body into the passenger seat. She didn't seem to mind my driving her new car. I aimed the silver rocket back to the resort, getting a feel for its breathtaking acceleration. *Da buggah fly!*

Pulling into the resort, I skipped the valets and parked the car myself in a dim corner of the lot. I slipped her keys into my pocket and helped the weaving Lani up the elevator and into my suite.

Inside she stumbled into the bedroom and fell onto the king-sized bead, sprawling there with a naughty-girl look on her face.

She giggled, kicked off her sandals, and fumbled with the zipper of her black cocktail dress.

"I shooo yooo a good time . . ."

twenty-nine

Lani made a "come hither" gesture with her little finger. I played along, helping with her zipper and slipping off my aloha shirt. I rolled back the bedspread, then the blanket and top sheet. She squirmed out off her dress.

I wondered what the thin man, no doubt listening in through the woodwork, would expect from us. Groans and moans and banging on the wall?

"Roll over on your tummy," I said to Lani.

"Yess, yess . . ." She quickly turned over. She had a body to die for. Too bad I wasn't ready to die.

I grabbed a bed pillow, removed its case, and twisted it into a rope. I slipped the fabric into her mouth.

"Wasss going on . . ."

I tied the pillowcase behind her shimmering black hair before she could finish her muffled sentence. Then I unplugged the phone cord and bound her hands and feet behind her, snug but not painfully tight. She could sleep on her stomach comfortably enough all night until she was found the next morning.

"Ahhh!" Lani tried to scream, without much effect. The result was a muted cry such as the thin man next door no doubt expected to hear. I let out a few lusty groans myself and rocked the bed against the wall for good measure.

Next I searched Lani's black sequined handbag. Soon I found her lipstick and makeup kit, carrying them and her black cocktail dress into the bathroom.

Ten minutes later, I emerged looking like a woman—sort of. I had put on lipstick, blusher, and eye shadow and had donned Lani's bra, stuffed with toilet tissue, and her black dress. Next I put on the lady's sun hat I had bought and tied the scarves under my chin. Fortunately, I'd brought a pair of rubber slippers that would have to do with my costume. I stuffed my own clothes and my files from the case into Lani's large handbag

Before leaving the suite, I glanced again at Lani. The *'ono* local beauty lay naked on the bed. Her glistening eyes looked at me with a doleful expression.

I covered her with the top sheet and blanket, then whispered in her ear: "Sorry, Lani. Your friend Manny has gotten mixed up in some nasty business. By Friday you'll know what it's all about. Sleep well."

I fluffed a pillow under her head and tiptoed from the room, locking the door behind me.

The silver Porsche opened remotely with Lani's key and I slipped into the driver's seat. The turbo motor fired with a throaty growl as I aimed toward Kona on Ali'i Drive. A mile down the road I pulled off to consult Lani's map. There is no direct route from Kona to Hilo. The high ridge between Mauna Loa and Mauna Kea separates the two towns. The shortest route—85 miles—climbs east over the remote Saddle Road between the two volcanoes. Since at night this narrow mountain pass can be tricky, it seemed prime turf for another one of the *hui's* accidents. A longer route, the Hawai'i Belt Road, stretched north through *paniolo* country to Waimea, then turned south down the rugged Hāmākua Coast. But if the *hui* was watching the remote Saddle Road, they would likely be watching the Belt Road, too. That left the longest route to Hilo—120 miles—weaving through the coffee groves of South Kona, around the southern tip of the island, and up into Volcanoes National Park. Would the *hui* figure on my taking this long and circuitous route? I hoped not.

The Porsche's clock said 8:29, less than two hours until the last flight to Maui. Before me lay the dark two-lane Kuakini Highway curving along the Kona Coast. Stars spread like crystal dust across the sky. I revved through the Porsche's lower gears, relishing the musical notes of its turbocharged motor at red line. Almost instantly I was over the speed limit.

I checked the rearview mirrors. Empty as the night. Few cars plied the highway on this starry Wednesday. But I stayed hyperalert, checking the speedometer, whose needle on the straightaways swept to 100. Checking mirrors. Checking the fuel gauge. Adrenaline pumping.

The village of Captain Cook blinked by as the highway rose gradually through the leeward hamlets of Kainaliu and Kealakekua, into South Kona coffee country. The Porsche's powerful high beams illuminated the narrow, twisting lanes in front of me, carving through desolate lava flows. I checked the mirrors again.

A flashing blue light.

No way could I pull over tonight. I was traveling at twice the speed limit in a borrowed car, lamely disguised as a woman.

The cop would stop me and lock me up. I would miss that Maui flight.

No way.

When the darkened highway swung east near the Big Island's southern tip, on a straight stretch through Hawaiian Ocean View Estates I put the pedal down. The speedometer quickly swept past 100. Then 120 . . . 140 . . . .

I was still flying when I reached the southernmost town on the island, Nāʻālehu. "35 mph" was the posted limit. I blew by at 135. I checked the mirrors. The blue light was gone.

Climbing the long grade into Volcanoes National Park in a sudden downpour, I thought about Manny and his twisted idea of ʻohana. By returning to Honolulu before the Zoning Board hearing on Friday I would be betraying him. By exposing the hui, if I got that far, I might tarnish his new, clean image. Or maybe put him behind bars.

Trying to save the cliffs was the right thing, the only thing, to do. If Manny perceived this as a violation of loyalty to family—ʻohana—he was wrong. Loyalty to the land—ʻāina— should be higher.

The landing lights of a distant jet illuminated Hilo Bay. Hilo International Airport—the sign loomed ahead on the drenched highway and none too soon. The rain cooperatively cut back to a mist, then stopped. I pulled into the parking lot with little time to spare, locked Lani's very warm Porsche, kept the keys in case I needed them later, and hurried to the terminal.

At the ticket counter, the agent did a double take when she saw my disguise. Was I a harmless cross-dresser? Or was I dangerous? I explained that I was flying to a costume party on Maui and didn't have time to change there. She bought my story, checked my ID, and sold me a ticket.

I walked away from the counter, fast enough to catch the plane but not to call attention to my pitiful self. An airport clock said 10:15. Ten minutes to departure.

When I finally reached the gate the agent announced: "Last call for flight 946 to Kahului, Maui. All ticketed passengers should be onboard."

I scanned around the passenger lounge. No police. And no one suspicious enough to represent the *hui.*

I handed my coupon to the agent and stepped down the jetway. The Boeing 737 was less than half full. Passengers were scattered randomly among many empty seats. I commandeered a row of three all to myself, and watched as the plane pushed back from the gate. The window reflected back my disguise— smeared lipstick, frowzy eyes, blushing cheeks.

Soon the jet turbines were humming and the terminal was shrinking away from my window. With little air traffic this late, the pilot taxied directly to the runway and revved the big fans as we thundered into the darkness over Hilo Bay.

thirty

Before dawn the next morning the ripsaw whine of a Twin-Otter jolted me awake. It was Thursday. Kahului Airport, Maui. Twenty-four hours to the Kalaupapa Cliffs hearing on O'ahu.

I uncurled from the vinyl chair that had been my bed for the night in the passenger lounge. My mouth tasted fuzzy. My back ached. My head pounded. But I had eluded the *hui*. So far.

Before going to sleep last night I had re-dressed as a tourist, complete with sunglasses purchased at an airport gift shop and a weathered L.A. Dodgers baseball cap I had bought from a genuine tourist for thirty bucks. I had heaped Lani's things and my Kalaupapa Cliffs files into a duffel, also purchased from the gift shop. Lipstick and eye shadow removed, once again I traveled as a man.

The 6:00 a.m. Twin-Otter flight I awaited offered two advantages: one, it was the first plane of the morning from Maui to Honolulu; and, two, it would arrive at the remote Island Hopper building, distant from the Inter-Island Terminal serving the larger jets from Kona and Hilo, which was no doubt being watched by the *hui*. That my flight first stopped on Moloka'i was not my choice. Though at this point I had few choices.

The tiny airplane puttered on to the runway, throttled up, and climbed into the dawn. The plane banked over Kahului Bay, skirted the gently sloping hills of West Maui, and crossed the channel between Maui and Moloka'i.

Four passengers got off at Moloka'i and three more climbed on for the short leg to Honolulu. Soon the Twin-Otter was airborne again. The pilot swooped over the majestic Kalaupapa cliffs, aglow in the early morning light.

It had been two weeks since Adrienne hired me to investigate her sister's death. Justice for Sara is what she had wanted. A seemingly straightforward request.

But the investigation had unearthed a conspiracy at the very root of island government. To ensure approval of the Kalaupapa Cliffs project despite overwhelming opposition, the *hui* had stopped at nothing. Sara's death, the original focus of the case, now served as only one tragic example of Chancellor Trust's ruthlessness. Today they were close to victory. The Land Zoning Board was about to approve their project. Unless I could stop them.

The Twin-Otter touched down in Honolulu at 7:10 and taxied to the Island Hopper terminal. When the pilot shut down the screaming turbines, I quickly squeezed out the door. Ducking behind another passenger walking to the quiet terminal, I looked around. No one seemed to notice me.

My Smith & Wesson. It lay at the bottom of a trash receptacle in the Inter-Island Terminal, which was surely being watched. I walked there quickly. I didn't see any *hui* operatives as I slipped into the restroom.

A man with a dirty yellow beard stood at the sink brushing his teeth. I stood by the stainless waste container and turned on the faucet. Without removing my baseball cap I washed my face, shiny with sweat. My cheeks were darkened with stubble. I wished I could brush my teeth. But more than that, I wished he would finish so I could retrieve my gun.

Finally the man gathered his toilet bag and left. I reached down under the trash liner. It was there—a cold, heavy lump. I slipped the revolver into my duffel and left the restroom.

In front of me was one of Bobo's moke pals. But his dark eyes were glued to the arrival gates. *Had he spotted me?* I turned and put some distance between us, then glanced back. He was still there, still watching the gates intently.

I walked briskly from the terminal. My duffel felt heavier with the Smith & Wesson aboard. A quarter mile ahead on the corner of Aolele Street and Nimitz Highway rose the airport Holiday Inn. It was morning rush hour, seven thirty, and town-bound traffic choked Nimitz.

I crossed the street and glanced back. Still nobody.

Before 8:00 a.m. may seem an odd hour to check in to a hotel, but not in Hawai'i. I told the front desk clerk I had just flown in from Auckland on Air New Zealand, stopping over in Honolulu before returning to Los Angeles. My Dodgers cap corroborated my story.

"Very good, sir." The aloha-shirted clerk smiled blandly.

With room key in hand I stopped by the lobby gift shop and bought disposable razors, a gaudy aloha shirt displaying hula dancers and waving palms, and a straw hat who band said "Hawai'i Paradise."

By 8:30 I was showered and dressed and calling the FBI. Agent Javier's phone just rang. *Damn!* I mentally prepared a message for his voice mail. Then I heard, "Javier, FBI."

"Bill, did you receive the fax from Bio-Tech Labs in California?"

"Yeah," Javier said. "What's this about? We don't usually investigate dead mules."

Briefly I explained the Kalaupapa Cliffs conspiracy and how the Chancellor Trust *hui* had run down Adrienne and killed Sara and her student, Baron Taniguchi.

"Kalaupapa Cliffs?" Javier pondered. "I read about that in the morning paper. The Land Zoning Board hearing is tomorrow, right?"

"That hearing has to be stopped."

"Why?"

"It's rigged. I'll have the evidence at your office by noon. If I don't show, take a look at my safe deposit box at First O'ahu Savings on King Street."

"In thirty minutes I can have a car there to pick you up, Kai."

"Can't risk waiting, Bill. If you want to help, alert the U.S. Attorney's Office that you'll be requesting an injunction suspending that Zoning Board hearing tomorrow. We need to work fast."

"Where are you? Let me send a car."

"See you at the federal building." I hung up.

thirty-one

"8:41" flashed on the marquee at the airport Holiday Inn. I stood at a bus stop on Nimitz Highway gripping my duffel with both hands. Though the bus is not the fastest way to travel, I knew I couldn't call a cab. The *hui* could be monitoring the cabbies' dispatcher.

In my campy aloha shirt and wide straw hat I felt anonymous among the locals and few tourists waiting for the bus. Finally, I saw two buses in the distance slowly rolling down the street, heading for our stop. One had "Waikīkī" printed across the front, the other "Ala Moana Center."

I shifted weight from one foot to the other. I looked up at the marquee: "8:45." When I looked back at the street, I saw something I wish I hadn't. The smoke grey van was parked at the opposite curb. *Damn!*

The buses pulled between us, blocking my view. I jumped on the Ala Moana bus and held my breath as it chugged away. The Waikīkī bus followed close behind. Glancing back, I saw the van swing an illegal U-turn on Nimitz. *Had the driver seen which bus I boarded?* Before long the two buses would split off in different directions and the van would have to make a decision.

When that happened, the van followed the Waikīkī bus. I could breathe again. As the van turned away, I saw only two men through the windshield. Neither was Bobo. That meant that he was still out there somewhere looking for me.

The bus traveled along Dillingham Boulevard, then turned onto King Street in Chinatown, rumbling past sidewalks stacked high with crates of bok choy and eggplant and bean spouts. At the corner of King and Nuʻuanu I stepped off the bus. First Oʻahu Savings was just opening. The assistant manager did a double take when she saw my oversized hat and splashy aloha shirt.

"On a case today, Kai?"

I winked and asked for my safe deposit box. She led me to a private booth, where I removed all the pieces of evidence from my box—the syringes, fingerprint cards, photos, Sara's speech, and the taped conversation with McWhorter. I slipped them into my duffel.

From the bank, I walked *makai* on Fort Street, a pedestrian mall whose cliff-like towers made for a shadowy promenade. The Federal Building on Punchbowl was only a half mile away. If the van showed, those mokes would have to chase me through the maze of shops and shoppers.

At the end of dusky Fort Street, the Aloha Tower glowed in the morning sun. Around the tower, boutiques and bistros and beer gardens bustled in the marketplace. I turned onto Ala Moana Boulevard and could spot the Federal Building only a half block away.

A flame red sports car suddenly flashed in the sunlight as it raced down Punchbowl, coming toward me fast. The car was low-slung. Italian. All too familiar. The plates said "Manny."

Both doors of the red Lamborghini swung up bizarrely like opening jackknifes. Manny stepped out and onto the sidewalk. His pal Bobo joined him.

"You betray me, Kai," Manny said. "I save your life and you spit in my face . . ."

Big Bobo didn't wait for Manny's speech to end. I ran back down Ala Moana Boulevard toward the Aloha Tower, with Bobo steps behind. Bobo ran fast for a big man, like an angry bear. I hoped I could lose him in the marketplace.

I sprinted across six lanes of traffic on Ala Moana, dodging cars, the Aloha Tower firmly focused ahead of me. I raced as fast as my feet would carry me, through the parking lot, past a line of yellow cabs, and by boutiques and browsing tourists.

Bobo kept pace. Since I was lugging my duffel, the big moke was able to stay with me. I was almost at the piers now, beyond the tower, which were blocked by an iron gate. I ran up the tower steps.

Bobo climbed after me, his huge feet pounding the spiraling stairway like thunder. I glanced back and saw that he clutched something dark in his meaty right hand.

Pop! I felt a rush of air as a bullet ripped into the stairwell above me. Splinters flew.

A woman screamed as Bobo pushed her aside. *Pop!* Another shot exploded like a mousetrap being sprung.

The searing heat of a fire iron tore into my left shoulder. I grabbed the place where blood was already seeping through. I tried to squeeze away the pain.

I hunched down on a landing, my aloha shirt dripping blood. With my right hand, I fumbled with the zipper of my duffel and finally made out the cold lump of my Smith & Wesson. I shook it free of the bag and lifted it to meet Bobo's gun. He paused, pistol pointed up the stairwell, as I aimed low and squeezed off two rounds.

The big man jolted back, clutching his stomach. He buckled over and tumbled. His gun clattered down the stairs.

I lunged past him toward the foot of the tower, where a flock of tourists had crowded the entrance. Pushing through them, I ran for the first yellow cab in the line.

I hopped in, slamming the door behind me. "Federal Building," I ordered the driver

Ten minutes later, I was knocking at the door of Agent Bill Javier.

thirty-two

"Feds Probe Kalaupapa Cliffs." Friday's *Star-Bulletin* detailed a wide-ranging federal investigation into Umbro Zia and the Chancellor Trust's *hui*. It was alleged that the trust had conspired to bribe members of the Land Zoning Board and other public officials by offering financial interest in the proposed resort. *Hui* members were also being questioned in the deaths of Baron Taniguchi and Sara Ridgely-Parke, and Adrienne's hit-and-run accident in Waikīkī.

Several suspected *hui* members were named, including Zia, Dr. Goto, Rush McWhorter, and Manny Lee. Jailed *Pakalōlō* King Milton Yu was not mentioned. Nor were Emery Archibald, Heather Linborg, or J. Gregory Parke. Somehow this made the wealthy Parke seem all the more forlorn.

The article explained that a federal judge had enjoined the Land Zoning Board from meeting, pending the outcome of the investigation. An accompanying editorial noted that the Chancellor Trust's proposal to develop eighty acres of Moloka'i conservation land–all but certain of passage yesterday–was now dead.

I reached up and touched my shoulder. Still pain. But the wound had been superficial, and was cleaned and bandaged that same afternoon. The emergency room physician had warned me to keep it out of the water for a few days. *Right.* If there was one thing I needed most in the world right now, it was surfing.

Late Friday morning, with agent Javier in tow, I visited Adrienne at the medical center. She had awakened from her long sleep and was speaking again, though faintly. To the agent, she corroborated much of what I had said about the *hui's* involvement in Sara's death.

After Javier had spoken with Adrienne a few minutes, he left us alone. Her newly regained voice began to fade.

"Save it." I took her hand. She looked so much better, I couldn't help wondering aloud if she would return to Boston immediately. Adrienne slowly shook her chestnut hair, glinting red and gold in the morning sun streaming through her hospital window. She squeezed my hand.

On my way back to my apartment that afternoon, I took a detour in Waikīkī and found myself barefoot with my board on a sun-warmed stretch of sand. Within minutes I was paddling out to Pops. My shoulder stung a little when I stroked, and even more with the first spray of salt water. Then the frothing soup from an inside set suddenly tore off my bandage. By the time I had reached the lineup, my shoulder was numb. But I felt alive. Restored. Balanced. And ready for the next wave.

The Making of *Murder on Moloka'i*
includes unpublished excerpts from the novel
by Chip Hughes

I began writing Murder on Moloka'i *in 1995. The book went though more than twenty complete drafts before it was published almost a decade later in 2004. The early drafts ran as long as 75,000 words, or close to four hundred pages. The finished product, barely 40,000 words and two hundred pages. Obviously, a lot was condensed and cut. This was done in an attempt to create a spare and compact novel. Though the bulk of the deleted material no doubt deserved to be cut, some passages that developed the character of Kai Cooke and the atmosphere of his life and his Hawai'i were also sacrificed. Not to mention an entire subplot concerning another case Kai was working when the Moloka'i investigation began. Some of this material appears below, along with brief explanations as to where and how it would have fit into a longer book. While most excerpts have never appeared in print before, readers familiar with* Murder on Moloka'i *may recognize some passages in their earlier guises. I have resisted the temptation to edit. The following pages are presented not as finished work, but as drafts. My purpose is rather to suggest other directions the novel might have taken and the various steps in the creative process.*

I: Early Beginnings: First draft, 1995

The first draft of Murder on Moloka'i *represents my
earliest conception of the character of Kai Cooke (originally
called "Keahi"). My fledgling emulation of the hard-boiled
school of Hammett and Chandler can be seen in phrases like
"heavy assignment," and trailing people "who might be trouble,"
and "protecting [one's] flesh." Kai's Smith & Wesson begins
here as a .38 snub-nose hammerless revolver, but later becomes
a .357 Magnum. Note the emphasis on the gun itself. Soon
I realized what set Kai apart from other fictional PIs was not
his firearm, but his surfboard. In recent years more gumshoes
who surf have appeared, but none to my knowledge for whom
wave riding is so central to every aspect of their character.
In this draft, Kai says his firm's name—Surfing Detective—is
merely a gimmick, whereas in later versions he tells us riding
waves actually helps him solve cases. Finally, the lines below
about his logo and his being mistaken for a celebrity did make
it into book at the end of chapter one.*

one

(1995 draft)

I keep a .38 snub nose revolver in the trunk of my car, unloaded. It's a hammerless Smith and Wesson, which when carried can be drawn and fired quickly. No private detective in Hawai'i is licensed to carry a concealed weapon. Being caught with one earns two years in jail. So when I go out on a heavy assignment, when I'm tailing someone who might be trouble, I weigh the benefits against the risks. Is protecting my flesh worth doing a couple years' time? Or, does staying out of jail merit taking a slug? It's a delicate balance. My job is full of delicate balances.

I'm Keahi Cooke. My business card says: "CONFIDENTIAL INVESTIGATIONS–ALL ISLANDS." Next to these words is my company logo–a lone surfer riding a wave. The same logo has appeared in the Honolulu yellow pages for the past six years. The surfer has nothing to do with my present occupation. I chose it as a gimmick to help clients remember me, and to recall my feats as a long board champion. I use the word "champion" broadly. When twenty-five, nearly a decade ago, I placed third in a local contest up at Pipeline. The trophy still sits on my Maunakea Street office, a little tarnished. Nonetheless, the gimmick has worked. Potential clients often ask, "Are you the surfing detective?"

My notoriety also has it drawbacks. Hardly a week goes by without a crank call. Celebrity seekers, bleary-eyed from reruns of *Hawaii Five-0,* sometimes phone my office for Jack Lord. This mystifies me. With sun-bleached hair and brown eyes I look nothing like Lord, nor from the reruns I've seen did he ever surf. I also get calls for Magnum P.I. When I was working late one night a breathy female voice asked if I was Tom Selleck. I forced myself to choke out, "No."

As I was saying, the .38 snubnose can get me out of trouble, but also get me into it. Therefore, I use the revolver sparingly.

II: New Beginnings: People are like waves

In 1998 the Jellinek & Murray Literary Agency of Honolulu circulated the first version of Murder on Moloka'i offered to publishers. This version begins with Kai expounding his view of human nature ("People are like waves") and introducing himself and his Surfing Detective agency. In subsequent drafts this three-page monologue was dismantled, revised, and moved to various other places in the book, finally coming to rest in chapter ten. In its original form the monologue shows how Kai's character evolved from the early drafts to the finished product. Notice that he starts now with waves, rather than guns. And while his gun does appear later, it rides in the car with his surfboard, the fragrance of whose coconut-scented wax he much prefers to the gunmetal and machine oil odor of the Smith & Wesson. He also says that using the word surfing in his firm's name is "no gimmick," in contrast to the first draft. And there is less hard-boiled talk than before.

one

(1998 draft)

People are like waves. On the surface they may appear turbulent or calm, but what really matters lies below. The most beautiful glassy tube, you see, can be the most dangerous. Under that luminous green barrel hides a jagged reef–just inches beneath the surface–that can rake the unsuspecting surfer like a cheese grater. Mushy beach break may pose less risk, but for *Pure Stoke* can't match the awesome tube.

Like waves, people present themselves in many guises. Whether surfing or working a case, I keep my eyes open. *Check out da reef, brah!* I scan the sea for saw-toothed coral. I survey the soup for uncharted boulders. I also scout the telltale fin of the tiger shark. Otherwise, by now I'd be a *dead* surfer. And a dead detective.

When I'm working I pack a .38 snub-nose revolver by my surfboard wax in the trunk of my Impala. The gunmetal and machine oil smell of the Smith & Wesson, magnified by the Hawaiian sun, almost reeks beside the sweet, coconut-scented paraffin. The blue black .38–gunmetal stink and all–is a necessary evil of my job. Me, I prefer the tropical scent of the surfboard wax.

I bought the hammerless .38 because I can draw and fire it quickly. My fast draw has drilled dozens of make-believe men at the Koko Head Range, and one flesh and blood man in the streets of Honolulu. The latter was an "armed and dangerous" (but not too smart) escaped con, trying to settle a score. It's a case I'd just as soon forget, since he nearly landed me in prison, if not at the undertaker.

Problem is, no private detective in Hawai'i is licensed to carry a concealed weapon. Getting caught with one earns the unlucky P.I. two years in jail. So when I go out on a heavy assignment, when I'm tailing someone who might be trouble, I weigh the benefits against the risks. Is protecting my hide worth doing a couple years' time? Or does staying out of jail merit taking a slug? It's a delicate balance. My job is full of delicate balances.

I'm Kai Cooke. *Kai* in Hawaiian means "sea." I was named after my Uncle Kaipo, an expert waterman who sailed Polynesia in a double-hulled koa canoe. My business card says "SURFING DETECTIVE" and "Confidential Investigations—All Islands." Above these words is my company logo—a longboard rider with toes on the nose. This "hanging ten" surfer is a thing of beauty: back gracefully arched, knees bent slightly, arms cantilevered behind for balance, gauzy ocean spray enveloping board and surfer like a white lace curtain. *Radical.*

An artist friend modeled the logo after an unknown wave rider at the Banzai Pipeline. My surfer logo has appeared in the Honolulu yellow pages for the past six years. This is no bogus gimmick. I really do surf. In fact, it wouldn't stretch the truth too much to call myself a longboard champion.

Well, *former* champion. When I was twenty-five, nearly a decade ago, I placed third in a local contest at Mākaha. The infamous Mākaha "bowls" were cranking up in the final round to twelve feet. *And higher.* Boards were snapping like toothpicks. I got lucky. One teeth-rattling ride positioned me to win it all. Then on the wave of the day—the wave *of my life*—I kicked out to rescue a fellow surfer hit by his board going over the falls. Neither of us won first prize. But my third-place trophy, tarnished by the years, still sits in my Maunakea Street office and holds special meaning.

More to the point, the surfer logo has worked. Potential clients may forget my name, but not the Surfing Detective.

III: Chapters One though Four: The Deadbeat Dad

*Once Kai's "People are like waves" monologue was removed
from the first pages of the 1998 draft, the revised first chapter
began with the discarded subplot mentioned above. This
subplot involves a deadbeat dad named Leonard Souza whose
wife has retained the Surfing Detective to collect delinquent
child support. Souza has not only failed to support his own
children, but has also taken up with barely a child himself,
cohabiting with her in a rusting fishing boat at the Ala Wai
Yacht Harbor in Honolulu. The confrontation that results
when the PI serves papers on the deadbeat was intended
as a day-in-the-life vignette. But it was thought to draw
away too much attention from the main plot. The piece was
later published as a short story entitled "Hijinks Aboard the
Hōkūlani" in* Spirit of Aloha *(March / April 2008), the in-
flight magazine of the now defunct Aloha Airlines, and in a
double issue of* Hawai'i Review: A Special Tribute to Ian
MacMillan *(Vol. 28-9; No. 1-2; 2008). Note that in this
early draft Kai was not merely* hānaied, *as in the published
version, but is part-Hawaiian. And that his attorney friend is
named not Tommy, but Harry.*

one

(1998 draft, revised)

Wednesday, October fourth.   Six a.m.   Ala Wai Yacht Harbor.

I was on a stake out by Waikīkī's famed Ilikai Hotel, atop whose aqua towers Jack Lord posed for the opening sequence of *Hawaii Five-O.* In my memory I could almost see the famous cascading wave that started the show and hear the drum roll and twanging guitars of The Ventures, as Lord's character, Detective Steve McGarrett, turned steely eyes to the camera.

My assignment this morning lacked the glamour of most of McGarrett's. (Glamour would arrive later in the day.) I was tracking a deadbeat dad named Leonard Souza. Souza and his seventeen-year-old girlfriend, a high school truant named Lei, were shacking up in a fishing boat called the *Hōkūlani.* A friend of the truant girl aboard had told me she was pregnant. That's why she didn't return to school.

Wackos.   Where do they all come from?   And slimy deadbeats. The *Hōkūlani,* it turned out, wasn't even Souza's.

From what I could gather, the dilapidated boat's absentee owner allowed him to live on board in exchange for making repairs. He and his seventeen-year-old baby-sitter got themselves a love nest, though a foul one, rent free. I could see no evidence from my stakeout position of any repairs to this rust bucket.

In my lap lay the manila envelope I had come to put into Souza's hands. It contained a court order—more precisely, a "Motion and Affidavit for Post-Decree Relief"—compelling him to appear at Family Court. A year behind on his child support payments, Souza had violated the terms of his divorce decree.

Several days of turning over rocks led me here to the yacht harbor at this ungodly hour, hoping to catch Souza off guard and deliver the affidavit. I was being cagey because his former wife had warned me in pidgin: "Leonard *like beef*." Meaning: If provoked, he could get nasty.

Mrs. Souza, his ex, was my client. I should never have taken her on. She couldn't afford my hourly minimum. She called me daily, sometimes twice a day. But how could I not feel sorry for her? She and her three kids were about to lose their home. So I made my habitual mistake.

"Avoid getting emotionally involved," all my P.I. training taught me. Trouble is, I'm a soft touch. My father's missionary ancestry and my mother's Hawaiian *aloha* compel me to lend a hand to every hard luck case that knocks at my door. Though my parents died long ago, their influence remains. Thus, I've helped my share of penniless clients and gotten sucked into some unprofitable, not to mention dangerous, cases.

Serving papers on hostile deadbeats like Souza can be a dicey business. My favorite strategy is to play dumb: I don't mention what's in the envelope until it's safely in the bad guy's hands.

Though I'd never admit to deliberately misleading anyone, sometimes my subjects get the mistaken idea that they're about to win the lottery or receive a check from an anonymous benefactor or a reward for a good deed done long ago but not forgotten. Once the court order has been duly served, I mention this disagreeable fact on my way out. By the time any tempers flare, I'm heading for the surf.

Aside from an occasional glitch, this strategy works. *Usually.*

two

(1998 draft, revised)

Soon the rising sun cast its mango hue on two snapshots Mrs. Souza had given me: one of her ex-husband, the other of the baby-sitter.

Leonard Souza was a scurvy looking fish with *salt-n-peppa* whiskers and shadowy circles under his charcoal eyes, the kind of scum you'd want to keep miles from your sister or daughter or girlfriend. Lei's picture, autographed in her feminine teenaged hand "To Mr. & Mrs. Souza," must have been taken at her junior prom. She wore an orchid corsage, frilly mauve dress, and an innocent smile. On her beauty-shop bun perched a rhinestone crown. *Queen for a day.* She was girlishly slim, with the telltale curves of a blossoming woman. Her pimple-faced boyfriend stood two inches shorter than his queen. From the nervous look in his eyes, she was obviously too much for him. Way too much.

I looked up. Nothing doing on Souza's boat. To stave off hunger and tedium I sucked on my favorite "crack seed," a local delicacy. "Sweet Li Hing Mui" is a pungent, sweet-sour plum seed that puckered my lips with such intense flavor that I quickly forgot my appetite and boredom.

Glancing again at the morning paper, I flipped to the weather page to check out the waves. Despite the confused shark at Laniākea who once mistook me for his lunch, I ride my longboard every chance I get. Surfing relieves the stresses of detective work and helps me explore the delicate balances that make up my job.

Sherlock Holmes had his pipe–I have my surfboard. Floating on the glassy sea, scanning the blue horizon for the perfect wave, sometimes I drift into a kind of trance. Then I can disentangle the most intricate web. When my wave finally rolls in, an instinct takes over. In one fluid motion I swing my board around, stroke like the wind, and rise. Slip-sliding down the thundering cascade–perched on a thin slice of balsa and foam–I find a precarious balance.

That's what surfing (and my job) is all about: *balance.*

The *Advertiser* forecast waves in Waikīkī at two to three feet. Elsewhere, a paltry flat to one. To Waikīkī I would go, once I served the affidavit on Souza.

Then I remembered a nine o'clock appointment with a woman from Boston whose name escaped me. I don't usually forget client names, but she had been referred during a long and rambling phone message from an attorney friend of mine.

"Oh, Kai, Ms. So-and-so from Boston may stop by . . . ," Harry had said offhandedly, as if he wasn't sure she would. Then he added cryptically: "If she shows, you'll be damn glad she did."

Whatever Harry's meaning, I was stuck with the appointment. Surfing would have to wait.

I glanced up again at the *Hōkūlani,* portholes still black as night. A typical stakeout. Sometimes I sit for hours sucking on my sweet-sour crack seed. But as I said, *balance* is the name of the game. Watching and waiting have to be as active as my moves, or I might miss something. Inevitably, when my vigilance slips, the case gets bungled. When my guard goes down, things turn dangerous.

So I stayed alert as I flipped pages in the *Advertiser—* from that chilling story about the plunging death from a mule of Sara Ridgely-Parke—to the sports pages, checking the baseball playoff scores and sumo standings from Japan.

After glancing at those alluring ads for tires and Korean hostess bars that follow sports—"ONO PUPUS & EXOTIC GIRLS!"—I turned to the business section and checked out an artist's sketch of a proposed Moloka'i resort called "Kalaupapa Cliffs." The resort loomed grand and blindingly white, an art deco Taj Mahal with marble spas and meandering pool and hundreds of ocean-view suites. "Kalaupapa Cliffs" promised to be a luxury palace designed for the super rich. *Like we really need one more of those!* Because of a technicality concerning the building site, the Moloka'i resort's construction awaited a vote of the Land Zoning Board.

Still no movement on Souza's boat. The climbing sun sent bars of intense light between Waikīkī high-rises, illuminating the drowsy harbor in jailbird stripes. Would Souza and his girl never crawl out of bed?

I started to worry that this stakeout might drag on into my nine o'clock appointment with the woman from Boston. It was now nearly seven thirty. An hour and a half had gone by and, although other fishing boats chugged one by one out to sea, on the *Hōkūlani* nothing had happened. Nothing.

If Souza didn't show his scurvy face pretty soon, I might have to start something.

three

(1998 draft, revised)

At twenty past eight, my patience wearing thin, a naked yellow bulb inside the slanting cabin of the *Hōkūlani* finally flashed on. Through the two portholes I saw movement. Tossing my crack seed into a planter of fragrant *lauwaʻe* ferns next to my teal Impala, I grabbed the manila envelope and strolled down the dock toward the rusty hulk.

My Dockers shorts, polo shirt, new pair of Raybans, and rubber *zoris* would have fit in well with the yachting crowd—had they been out of bed yet.

I wear a number of such outfits for protective coloration, trying not to stand out. At six feet even (well, almost) and one eighty, I have a fairly deep chest and well-developed shoulders and arms from surfing. Despite my year-round tropic tan, my skin looks light for a *hapa*. I seem to have inherited my sandy-haired father's fair complexion and my brown-eyed mother's Hawaiian soul. Truth is, she was one quarter Hawaiian, which makes me only one eighth.

So that Souza wouldn't get instantly suspicious, I folded and slipped the envelope containing the affidavit into my back pocket.

"'Morning," a sun-burned crewman said, mopping the deck of a spotless cabin cruiser.

"Howz'it?" I smiled and walked on. Beneath my feet that lime green sea lapped between planks in the dock. Sleek sailboats and motor yachts graced the countless slips.

Striding across the dock planks I wondered what Harry had said that Boston woman's name was. His message on my answering machine had been vague about why he referred her. Though I would have rather spent the morning surfing three footers in Waikīkī, I began to feel curious about this potential case. I don't get many clients from Boston.

The closer I got to Souza's listing craft, the worse it looked by comparison to its pristine neighbors. Soon I was standing near the two portholes that had appeared pitch black from my car. Now they were transparent. I caught a glimpse of the girl, who bore faint resemblance to her photo as prom queen. She wore only bikini panties and a sheer nightgown that stopped half way down her thighs. She was reed thin with little upturned breasts. The rounded bulge in her tummy confirmed what her high school friend had confided.

Behind the girl I saw the dark, whiskered man slipping on soiled denims and a black t-shirt with sleeves ripped out. Flecks of yellow-grey riddled his patchy beard and oily hair.

Scum. That's what flashed through my mind when I laid eyes on this cradle-robbing deadbeat. Even if Mrs. Souza could pay me nothing (a distinct possibility), I would relish busting up his scuzzy little boat party.

Since neither the girl nor Souza seemed in any hurry to leave their tiny cabin, I had to do something soon or stand up the woman from Boston.

The *Hōkūlani's* sloping aft deck offering neither boarding plank nor ladder, I climbed aboard over a gunwale onto the badly caulked teak. Two fishing poles mounted in chocks on either side of the stern had lines out in the water. One pole bobbed. On deck lay a long, hooked gaffe. The gaffe gleamed in the sun the like chrome bumper of my Impala and looked razor sharp.

I tapped on the cabin door. No answer. Though I'm a veteran at serving papers, a few butterflies fluttered in my stomach. I wouldn't exactly call this fear, just adrenaline. I knocked on Souza's door again.

Silence in the cabin.

"Hello!" I announced in perfect mainland English. "You've got a nibble on one of your lines."

The door opened and Souza swaggered out. He looked grubbier than his photo and he smelled rank, like stale sardines. A jagged scar, not visible in the snapshot, slanted up over his left eyebrow like a bent apostrophe. He'd been in a few *beefs,* all right. But despite my butterflies, he didn't scare me. I could handle him, though laying him out wasn't part of my job.

"Eh, brah!" Souza snarled. "What you doin' on my boat?"

"So sorry," I replied like a high-toned yachtsman. "Thought you might have a bite."

He eyed me suspiciously. The bobbing pole went slack. Souza had lost his fish.

"What do you catch in this harbor?" I pointed to the murky, lime-green water.

"*Kōkala*—Puffer Fish," he replied grudgingly. "Why you like know?"

I glanced on deck again at that gleaming, razor-sharp gaffe.

"Bettah get off da boat, eh?" Souza said. "My insurance no cover you." He turned toward the cabin.

"Another nibble!" I shouted. When he looked back at his poles I reached into my pocket and put the envelope in his hands.

"What dis, brah?" His coal eyes smoldered.

I glanced toward the dock, mapping my escape. Instinctively, my knees bent and my feet shifted, ready to jump. Once Souza saw the manila envelope he knew.

"*Fuckah!*" he shouted. "*You Fuckah!*" He dropped the envelope on the deck and, sure enough, grabbed that vicious-looking gaffe.

Before I could leap onto the dock, he swung the gaffe. The fastest way out was over the stern. *Bail out, brah! Bail!*

I dove down into the murky harbor as far from the boat as I could. But the gaffe came flying in after me, catching my right ankle. A sharp pain shot up my leg. I struggled under water, my polo shirt clinging like a wet blanket. My new Raybans sank into the murk. I kicked off my *zoris* and swam beneath the surface as long as my breath would hold. Behind me trailed a thin stream of blood. *Hungry sharks?* I wondered.

Coming up for air, I looked around to get my bearings. The *Hōkūlani* lay thirty feet away. My rubber *zoris* bobbed nearby on the water like two planks adrift. Souza glared at me from the stern.

"*Fuckah!*" He waved the court order angrily. The long legal pages flapped in the air.

I dove down deep and swam under water again. When I rose for another breath the rusty boat looked smaller, less menacing. Souza was nowhere in sight. I swam on the surface to the nearest dock, patting my shorts for my wallet and keys. Luckily neither had gone south with my sunglasses.

Climbing onto the dock planks I limped barefoot and dripping to my car. The *zoris* I simply left floating by the *Hōkūlani*. My bleeding ankle stung. Like a shallow coral cut, the wound thankfully went just beneath the surface.

At the harbor's edge I glimpsed again those aqua towers of the Ilikai Hotel where Jack Lord flashed his steely eyes at the opening of *Hawaii Five-0*. I tried to recall if his Detective McGarrett ever served papers on a deadbeat or got attacked by a gaffe. *Doubtful.* Or did I miss that episode?

I checked my watch. Quarter to nine. Fifteen minutes till my appointment. It would take me nearly that long in traffic to drive—soaked and bleeding—to my Maunakea Street office. Then ditch my sodden clothes.

I wished I'd never agreed to meet with that woman from Boston.

four

(1998 draft, revised)

My Impala crawled along the waterfront on choked Ala Moana Boulevard past the soaring Aloha Tower. Both long white hands of the tower's Big Ben-like clock, a dozen stories above the harbor, pointed to a black Roman nine.

Beneath the Aloha Tower the nautical flags of a Norwegian cruise ship–crimson, mustard yellow, and navy blue–barely rippled in the slack trades. My clothes dripped like wet laundry begging for the spin cycle. The beach towel I always carry for surfing lay under me drenched, not doing much to keep the driver's seat beneath it from growing soggier by the minute. Blood trickled from my stinging ankle. *Damn that Souza!*

I wasn't too happy about the salt water and blood dripping in my Impala. It's sort of a classic.

I bought the teal blue '69 Chevy from a widow whose late husband purchased it new at Aloha Motors, a defunct dealership formerly on the site of the Hawai'i Convention Center. With less than 50,000 original miles, the Impala's three hundred horse V–8 still really rocks. And with the back seat removed, my longboard slides right in.

Wheeling the Impala downtown between steel and mirror office towers that hid all but a sliver of the grass green Koʻolau Range, I wondered again about the woman from Boston. What did Harry mean: "If she shows, you'll be damn glad she did"? Despite my six years in the business I still feel a little queasy when meeting new clients. You never know what you'll get.

I turned onto Maunakea Street, a slice of old Honolulu bordering Chinatown's teeming, mismatched buildings and pungent aromas. Along the half mile the two-lane drag runs *makai,* or seaward, from Foster Botanical Gardens to the harbor, Maunakea intersects notorious Hotel Street—a strip of raunchy bars, porno houses, flea bag hotels, prostitutes, and drug dealers.

The boys in blue at the HPD sub-station try occasionally to weed out these bad elements, but they always spring back like the flamboyant night-blooming cereus up the street at the botanical gardens. Me, I don't mind. You'd be surprised how helpful these neighbors can be on certain cases.

Maunakea Street's hodgepodge of crumbling buildings brought to mind that young "Ecofeminist" attorney who had tragically lost her life on Molokaʻi. *What would she have thought of my funky digs?* This is not the part of town where you'd expect to find a P.I. with ambitions. Truth is, a half dozen years back when I was just starting out I had higher expectations. My first office in a swankier part of town—Bishop Street, no less—cost me most of what I could make. But that's another story. When I figured out I was giving up too much wave riding just to keep an address, I moved here to Maunakea.

Things are simpler now. These days I maintain only two rules for business: don't starve and don't get drilled. Oh, and a third rule for pleasure: *Plenny time fo' surf!*

At five minutes to nine I pulled into my garage, then hobbled shoeless and dripping along the crumbling sidewalk toward my office. Not wanting to keep a prospective client waiting, I started to jog. *Ouch!* My ankle stung. I slowed again to a hobble. Given the stares of passersby, I must have been a sight—even in this neighborhood. A homeless man curled on yellowed newspapers by a bankrupt cigar shop peered at me, rubbed his pink eyes, then spit in my direction. The urine reek of his grimy clothes quickened my halting pace up Maunakea.

My office is easy to find above the corner shop called Fujiyama's Flower Leis. Mrs. Fujiyama owns a decaying pre-war building at Maunakea and Beretania Streets that boasts dazzling ornaments of an Oriental cast—two-headed dragons, serpents, wild boars, and ancient Chinese characters spelling some (to me) mysterious message in red. The walls are riddled with enough cracks to keep a journeyman plasterer busy for months. The second, or top floor is divided into five tiny offices. Mine, the roomiest of the bunch, is a twelve-by-twelve cubicle with a window overlooking Maunakea Street.

Trailing drops of sea water into the flower shop, I searched among the refrigerated display cases for the woman from Boston. Plenty of ginger, plumeria, tuberose, *pīkake*, and orchid leis, but no sign of her. The vivid floral scent of the shop raised the hair on the back of my neck—making me feel sort of spiritual, or just plain *lōlō*.

Mrs. Fujiyama's establishment offers my clients both wonderful fragrances and a degree of anonymity. They can browse leisurely among the perfumy leis, then slip unnoticed upstairs. If detected, they can pretend to be patronizing one of the four other tenants: a free-lance editor, bookkeeper (who's never in), passport photographer, or Madame Zenobia, a psychic. I wonder sometimes if any of these businesses are fronts, though I've never bothered to check.

Fortunately, Mrs. Fujiyama didn't see me trail sea water across her scuffed brown linoleum. But her youngest lei girl, a Filipino college student named Chastity, did.

"Eh, Mr. Cooke," said Chastity, stringing a pale yellow plumeria lei, "You're so wet!"

"Dawn-patrol surfah." I winked and headed up the orange shag stairs past the glass bead curtain and locked door at Madame Zenobia's, who seldom does readings before noon.

The smoky veneer hallway was empty by my door that says "SURFING DETECTIVE" beneath the graceful longboard rider hanging ten—as on my business cards. I unlocked the two dead bolts and the heavy mahogany door creaked open. I put in this solid wood door and the dead bolts myself because Mr. Fujiyama, when he built these offices, used hollow-core doors with cheap knob-locks. The locks were a joke. A common kitchen knife could spring them. As for the hollow-core doors, a little *keiki*—a mere child—could easily punch a fist through.

The musty smell of the office floated through the opened door even before I stepped inside. But after my morning's swim, the familiar whiff and disorder of the place felt reassuring. Atop a filing cabinet across from my battleship grey desk stood a tarnished trophy: THIRD PLACE–CLASSIC LONG BOARD–MĀKAHA. My faded glory.

When I was twenty-five, nearly a decade ago, I won this trophy in a local contest at Mākaha. The infamous Mākaha "bowls" were cranking up in the final round to fifteen feet. *And higher.* Boards were snapping like toothpicks. I got lucky. One teeth-rattling ride positioned me to win it all.

Then on the wave of the day—the wave *of my life*—I kicked out to help a fellow surfer hit by his board going over the falls. Neither of us took home first prize that day. But the third-place trophy, tarnished now by the years, still sits above my filing cabinet.

I checked my watch again. *Five after nine.* Maybe the woman from Boston would be a few minutes late? I opened my lone office window, releasing the stale air, and took a quick look for her down on Maunakea Street. The sharp, competing smells of kim chee, espresso, rancid garbage, hot malasadas, and ginger leis wafted in.

Across from the flower shop stood an old porno theater, recently converted to a Christian radio station. Last week I'd watched the new owners take down from the marquee two spicy titles—"Hot Rackets" and "Debbie Does It Again"—replacing them with "JESUS COMING SOON." Nearby an old porno buff, unaware of the theater's conversion, hustled to the ticket booth with visions in his X-rated mind of the man from Nazareth I shudder to contemplate. Whatever the faithful inside told him, the porno buff stalked away dejected with fists thrust in his pockets like lead weights. He was upset. *Plenny* upset.

Now by this converted theater I saw no cab and no woman who looked like she came from Boston. I surveyed the surrounding businesses: Leong's Dry Cleaning, Taka's Antiques, and C & K Diner, where a buck fifty buys you a Spam *musubi* plate lunch. Near C & K's take-out window I spotted two more homeless men leaning on grocery carts piled high like container ships with worldly belongings, but no client.

Unlocking the filing cabinet that displays my tarnished longboard trophy, I pulled from the bottom drawer a pair of old Levi's I wear for dirty work and a Town & County Surf t-shirt.

My soaked clothes—underwear and all—I shed into a heap on the dusty linoleum. From the back of the file drawer I reached for a moldy hand towel and dried myself, hoping the woman from Boston didn't show while I was stark naked.

Three taps sounded at my door.

IV: Chapter Three: Paniolo Johnny Kaluna

I would be remiss if I did not provide at least one example of how editors can enormously improve a book. My wife, Charlene, read and commented on every draft. And Kirsten Whatley tightened the book into its final form. The finished product is much better because of their efforts, and those of specialist editors. Ku'ualoha Ho'omanawanui, Puhi Adams, Rodney Morales, and Scott Burlington, as mentioned in the acknowledgements, played a significant role in giving Murder on Moloka'i *an authentic island feel. Ku'ualoha, an Assistant Professor of English at the University of Hawai'i at Mānoa who holds the only faculty position dedicated to Hawaiian literature anywhere in the world, transformed the character of Johnny Kaluna. In chapter three when Kai meets Johnny, we are introduced to a genuine* paniolo, *or Hawaiian cowboy, who looks, speaks, and acts the part. It was not so in the first draft, before Ku'ualoha's magic touch. As can be seen in the excerpt below, the* panilolo's *name was originally Moreno, not Kaluna, he spoke in "proper" mainland English, rather than island pidgin sprinkled with Hawaiian phrases, and though he looked like a cowboy, he lacked such island touches as a red* palaka *shirt and skin tanned reddish brown like* koa. *Notice too that Kai himself spoke in formal English, rather than responding in kind to Kaluna's pidgin. The result was a formal and stilted exchange between the two men that Ku'ualoha helped to make more authentic.* Mahalo!

"Mr. Moreno?" I called.

No answer.

I looked at my watch. It was 7:30, the time we had appointed for our meeting. I heard a vehicle and walked back outside. It was a Jeep pickup, the bed filled with hay bails. A mustached man in a cowboy hat climbed out, skin tanned deeply like cherry wood. His jeans were worn white around the thighs—not fashionable faded, but really worn. A pair of riding boots and a western shirt with pearl buttons rounded out the effect. This man looked like a *paniolo*. We stood in the mist and introduced ourselves.

"Mr. Cooke?" He extended his right hand, his dark brown hair curling under the brim of his cowboy hat.

"Mr. Moreno, where are your mules?" I shook his hand.

"Gone to a west Moloka'i ranch," he said. "Gone until the lawyers draw up new papers."

"New papers?"

"Liability waivers for our mule riders to sign." His almond eyes looked wary. "Ever since that accident we've been temporarily shut down."

"Too bad," I said.

"Are you a lawyer, Mr. Cooke?"

"No, I'm a private investigator," I replied. "Don't worry, my client has no interest in suing your tour company."

Moreno seemed relieved. "There's not much work for me while we're shut down, except driving to the ranch twice a day to feed and water the mules"

"Tell me about the accident."

"It was the worst day of my life," Moreno said. "The young lady, Sara, she fell about three hundred feet into a gorge. There was a doctor in the party, but he couldn't do a thing. Not even help Coco."

"Who's Coco?

"A mule." Moreno's eyes glistened. "A damn good mule. Not like him to stumble. I buried him right by the trailhead. You'll see the wooden cross when we hike down."

"You buried the mule yourself?"

"He was my favorite." Moreno blinked, then rubbed his moist eyes. "Come on in." He motioned me toward the barn. "I'll get you the doctor's name and the others."

We walked into the tack room with the saddles and blankets and harnesses hanging on the wall. From the drawer of a small, dusty desk Moreno pulled out a guest book and opened it to a date in early September.

"This is the day," he said. "There were four riders besides the young lady who died. None of them seemed to know the others. One was the doctor. And there were two more men and a woman."

"May I copy their names and addresses?"

"Sure." He handed me the dusty book. The doctor whose name was Benjamin Ganjo kept his office in Honolulu. The woman, Heather Linborg, lived on Maui. The second man, Milton Yu, gave an address on the Hāmākua Coast of the Big Island. And the third man, Emery Archibald, listed only "Island Fantasy Holidays, Glendale, CA."

"What can you tell me about these four people?" I asked Moreno.

"That was a month ago," he said. "Usually I forget customers' faces after that long, but the accident, you know, kind of riveted me."

"I understand."

"The woman, Heather, was a nice-looking blond. Very nice. And young. In her twenties."

"Did she talk much with Sara?"

"Not that I recall," Moreno said. "Heather talked mostly with the local Chinese man, Milton Yu."

"What about this Archibald? Did he talk with Sara, or act strangely around her?"

"Oh, he talked with her, I'm sure. But no differently than anybody does on a mule ride. Just visited with her, if you know what I mean."

"And the doctor?" I asked.

"Same thing," Moreno said. "That Dr. Ganjo was on the heavy side. I gave him my biggest mule."

"Did the doctor make any attempt to help Sara when she fell?"

"There was no use," the mule guide said. "We couldn't reach her in the gorge."

I pulled out the photo Adrienne had given me of J. Gregory Parke and showed it to Moreno. "Have you ever seen this man?"

Moreno's almond eyes squinted. He twitched his mustache. "Yeah, I've seen him."

"You have?" I was stunned, but tried not to show it.

"He rode to Kalaupapa a day or two before the accident."

"Can you verify that?"

"By the guest book." He turned back one page to the day before Sara's fatal ride. "Here are the names. You can look for yourself."

Sure enough, on the list was "J. G. Parke." Could Adrienne have a case after all?

"Can you remember anything about Parke?" I asked Moreno.

"He's in his fifties, I'd say. Turning grey. Quiet. He seemed preoccupied," the mule guide said. "Didn't take much interest in the tour."

I put away the photo. "Can we hike down the trail now to see where Sara fell?"

"Sure." He took out a cash box. "Do you want to pay now or later?"

"Now is fine." I pulled out my wallet and handed him some bills.

"Sorry, I have to ask," Moreno said, "but I've got few customers since the accident, except hikers."

"No Problem."

V: Chapter Ten: Mauna Kea Takes Kai's Parents

In chapter ten Kai interviews witness Heather Linborg on Maui, then flies to the Big Island along the Hāmākua Coast to interview another witness, Milton Yu. Through the airplane's windows the PI watches Maui's Hāna Highway curve along the coast, reflects on his conversation with Lingborg, and then, as the Big Island comes into view, he spots Mauna Kea, Hawai'i's tallest mountain, which he describes as "cloud shrouded and dominating." In the earlier versions of the novel, seeing Mauna Kea prompted him to reflect on the accidental death of his parents on this mountain and how it changed his life. This excerpt contains details of Kai's childhood and his motivation for becoming a private detective—namely, to vindicate his father from causing the accident.

(cut from)
ten

At a few minutes past noon the Hilo-bound DC-9 rumbled over Kahului Bay. As the crowded liner banked southeast along Maui's Hāna coast, I had a moment to contemplate Heather Linborg. I couldn't get over her lie. Or her gold bikini.

Below the climbing jet, fabled Hāna Highway coiled along the twisting coastline. Deep emerald canyons of bamboo, breadfruit, and flowering *ōhi'a* were pierced by silver dagger waterfalls. I could see a sampling of the winding road's six hundred curves and hairpins, and fifty-odd bridges, knowing them all first-hand. As we glided over this craggy, foam-washed coast with majestic Haleakalā towering in the distance, I wondered if the Maui masseuse had served Parke in her professional capacity—a mere rub down?—or in some more personal way. That she knew him at all seemed ominous.

Remote Hāna Bay soon drifted under our wings, a tranquil azure pond bringing an end to Maui. Then nothing but sea green, a shade darker than Heather Linborg's eyes. The plane crossed the twenty-mile 'Alenuihāhā ("great billows smashing")

Channel to the island of Hawai'i. As I recalled from a boat passage once with my parents, this channel between Maui and its southern neighbor can get pretty wild. Today's flight was smooth. Not a single bump.

Soon the Big Island, twice the land area of all other Hawaiian islands combined, loomed ahead at its northern tip, the lush mountainous spine of North Kohala. The Maui masseuse slipped from my thoughts as we flew along Kohala's windward coast. *What a view!* Over on the lee slopes, fleetingly visible through cotton white clouds, lay the rolling green pastures of Parker Ranch. Down among the coastal lava beds sprawled the ocean-front fairways and velvet greens of the Mauna Kea and Waikoloa golf resorts. And on the windward side, directly beneath us, soaring sea cliffs were pierced by more silvery cascades.

As the jet descended south along the Hāmākua Coast, where soon I would interview Milton Yu, groves of kukui stood out like lime-green swatches against the darker green cliffs. The fire-orange flowers of African tulip trees dotted the landscape like a pointillist's canvas. Above these flamboyant trees rose Mauna Kea. I grimaced at the sight of this tallest mountain in Hawai'i—cloud-shrouded and dominating.

Mauna Kea, you see, took my parents' life. Their light plane crashed into the mountain when I was only eight. I can never look at Mauna Kea without thinking of them and how my fate suddenly and irrevocably changed. The accident report blamed pilot error. I never believed it.

The sky had been clear. My father was an experienced, careful pilot who knew every inch of Big Island terrain. Though the report exonerated the airplane's manufacturer and the firm from whom he leased it, I suspected some of the "investigators" had ties to these two entities. In any case, I received compensation from neither. A modest life insurance policy became my only legacy.

I had been an only child. Now I was alone. My cousin Alika's family, the Kealoha's of the North Shore, welcomed me into their *ohana* and treated me as their own. But since I was a shy boy raised in town and accustomed to the hallowed halls of Punahou, I had trouble adjusting to an unfamiliar public school. My grades fell. Through lengthy family negotiations I was too young to understand, it was decided that I would attend private school in California and live with the family of my father's brother, Orson T. Cooke of Pasadena.

I grew up with three sandy-haired cousins who looked like my brother and sisters. No one outside the family's rambling Tudor on a hillside cul-de-sac off Orange Grove Boulevard knew I was part Hawaiian. I spoke little pidgin. I shed my "Island-style" ways. Gradually I became a Californian.

Ironically, it was California—not Hawai'i—that kindled my passion for surfing. Cousin Matthew Cooke and I haunted our favorite spots: Malibu, Rincon, County Line, Trestles. After graduating from preppy Ridgecrest Academy, we trekked south to California Surfside College—a liberal arts school perched on Sunset Cliffs at Point Loma—boasting four of the best breaks in San Diego. At "Cal Surf," as students fondly dubbed our college, we clocked more hours in the water than in the classroom. I had a blast— until my father's life insurance ran out.

I quit the pricy beach-side school (against my Uncle Orson's advice) and joined the Army, after a recruiter promised me duty at Fort DeRussy in Waikīkī. *Shibai.* Didn't happen. I spent my whole tour stateside. When discharged I returned to San Diego intending to complete my degree with Army money at Cal Surf. Instead I partied and rode waves. Cousin Matthew, by then a management trainee at Acme Casualty, landed me a job as a claims adjuster.

I never did finish college. Claims work taught me volumes, however, about human nature. I witnessed more half-truths, deception, and outright fraud than I care to remember. This glimpse into the darker side prepared me—better than any classroom—for my later occupation.

People are like waves. Despite appearances, look out for what lies below.

Insurance investigation sharpened my instincts for sham. When I finally returned to Hawai'i I began gathering evidence on my parents' accident. Someday I will put all the pieces together. Though the statute of limitations may have expired, though I may never win a dime from the guilty parties, at least I will vindicate my father. Anyway, nothing could compensate for what I lost.

VI: Chapter Eleven: Toes on the Nose at Rock Piles

Before meeting his client Adrienne Ridgely for drinks at sunset at the Halekūlani in Waīkikī in chapter eleven, Kai paddles out to a surf break called Rock Piles. He's getting nowhere with the case at this point, or with his long-distance girlfriend, Niki, who lives in Los Angeles. Out in the water he's able to sift through the various pieces of the puzzle, and to contemplate the sad state of his love life. As part of the original conception of the series, I've tried to include scenes in each book showing Kai surfing and reflecting on his cases, and his life. "Sherlock Holmes had his pipe: I have my surfboard," says Kai in Murder on Moloka'i. *In the cut paragraphs below, while he does mention his client, a suspect he's about to interview, and a previous case, he focuses mainly on surfing itself — its dangers and rewards.*

(cut from)
eleven

Sunday afternoon before meeting Adrienne I looked at dismal apartments for rent, made more dismal by the fact that Niki hadn't popped into town for weeks. Later I tried calling her, but again got only her answering machine. Rather than break the good news that I might see her soon in Los Angeles, I decided to just drop in at her apartment in Marina Del Rey near the L.A. airport. If she was home, we'd have a surprise reunion. If not, the drive wasn't much out of my way.

Buoyed by the thought of seeing Niki I squeezed in a surf session before sunset at Rock Piles, offshore of the Ala Wai yacht harbor where I had tangled with that scurvy deadbeat, Leonard Souza. Rock Piles can be an especially good spot in summer—with hollow peaks and occasional tubes breaking over a shallow coral reef—but boards washed against the harbor's lava rock jetty can end up in splinters, not to mention surfers who ride them.

Surfing, like any sport, has its hazards. One wrong move on a winter swell at Waimea Bay, for instance, can ruin your whole day. The wave rider who wipes out on a smoking thirty-foot wall may stay under the white water for not seconds, but entire minutes. Or hours. The surfer's body floats ashore, or is never seen again. It depends. No one knows exactly why the drowned ones disappear, except maybe the sharks.

I was once asked to find the remains of such an unlucky waterman, a Californian reported missing after getting hammered one big December day at Waimea. His fractured board had rolled in, but not his corpse. It proved an eye-opening case, convincing this middle-aged longboarder to leave those North Shore titans alone.

Straddling my board at Rock Piles, waiting for one of those lovely peaks to form up, I puzzled over the case of Sara Ridgley-Parke. So far, no witness had admitted to seeing Sara fall, though each was covering up something. Only Archibald had been in a position to observe Sara's plunge. Would the travel agent shed light on the mystery? In Los Angeles I would soon find out.

Before long I spotted a clean set rolling in, swung my board around, and blissfully forgot Archibald. On the peaking left break, I planted a rail and turned hard to stay ahead of the curling lip. Trimming to a smooth plane, I cross-stepped forward gingerly, aping the tip-riding logo on my office door. *Toes on the nose!*

Just as my pinkies reached the tip, my longboard suddenly pearled (nose-dived) and I flipped *hulihuli,* head over heels. My board shot tail-first from the soup like a missile. Fortunately, it didn't hit me in the chops. I felt a big yank on my ankle as the ten foot leash snapped tight.

My caroming surfboard and I were safe, spared today from the lava rock jetty. But I had taken an embarrassing spill. Especially for a former champion.

Later I recouped. A few ripping good rides put me in the mood for dinner with Adrienne. At five o'clock I carried my board home, showered, dressed, and then walked back to the Halekūlani.

VII: Chapter Twelve: Kai's Shark Bite

The centrality of surfing to his character is brought home through Kai's frequent surf sessions, his surfboard always riding next to him in his car, and his using surfing as a metaphor for life and a way to solve problems and cases. But his ever-present badge of belonging as a surfer is the crescent of sixteen welts on his chest. He was attacked, as he tells us, one morning at Laniākea. A tiger shark bit him once and swam away. Kai unveils his shark bite in each book, typically in intimate moments. Below is one of those moments—cut from chapter twelve of Murder on Moloka'i *—in which Kai accompanies his client, Adrienne Ridgely, to her room after drinks at the Halekūlani Hotel. Following this is the sequel to the scene where he reminisces about his evening with her.*

(cut from)
twelve

Sometime during that evening, I forget exactly when, we ordered from room service Mumms champagne and a *pūpū* platter of seared *'ahi,* fried mozzarella, and sesame chicken in ginger sauce. Emboldened by the Mumms, Adrienne explored with tentative fingertips the crescent of pink welts on my chest. Each of the sixteen raised teeth marks she touched slowly, methodically—one at time.

"Oh, you poor thing!" She stood back and gazed at the half moon-shaped bite. "You *poor thing.*"

I let it pass.

Adrienne wasn't the first woman to touch my shark "trophy," but her warm, soothing caress penetrated like deep heat—down to that dark secret place where I had filed away and forgotten the attack. Her touch on those scars felt more intimate than our love making. *Why?* I had no wish to relive that morning at Laniākea. Being able to remember is a useful skill; being able to forget is better. *For real.* Otherwise, how could I ever surf again?

After the champagne and *pūpūs,* I left the Halekūlani at about three, stumbling back to my apartment through the drowsy, moonlit streets of Waikīkī.

Five hours later I dragged myself aboard a crowded DC-10 bound for Los Angeles. It was Monday, October 9. Booking the flight only the day before, I found myself sandwiched in the cramped middle section of the coach cabin. *Bummahs.* Every time I tried to snooze, another passenger crawled over me to stretch or use the lavatory and I awoke with an aching head and a guilty conscience.

My Technicolor dreams featured gauzy images of slender, supple Adrienne, her baby soft skin luminous in the buttery Waikīkī moonlight. I tasted again her sweet, coconut milk kiss–her deeply passionate kiss. This cool, crisp, headstrong woman from Boston had shown yet another side.

Two aspirin eased the throb at my temples, but did nothing for my nagging conscience. Here I was only hours from seeing Niki and I'd just slept with another woman.

VIII: Chapter Twelve: La Casa Nova

Later in chapter twelve, after interviewing witness and suspect Emery Archibald at his Glendale, California travel agency, Kai visits the apartment of his girlfriend, Niki, in Marina Del Rey, near the Los Angeles airport. Niki is not at home, but her other boyfriend is—an airline pilot named Jacoby. This is a sad revelation for Kai, but his just desserts, as he himself admits. Since he has just spent the night with his client, he is in no position to blame Niki for seeing someone else. The scene of his encounter with Jacoby that runs two pages in the published novel, extends to nearly six in the earlier drafts and contains numerous details and nuances cut from the book. Why was the scene cut? Perhaps because it develops Kai's character more than it contributes to the solution of the crime.

twelve
(longer version)

By ten that morning I was driving down Glenoaks Boulevard back to the Red Lion hotel. I gathered my things, checked out, and headed for L.A. International, retracing my path on the now less choked Ventura and San Diego Freeways. My flight to Honolulu departed at two, so I had plenty of time to surprise Niki and, if she was home, call the airline to extend my stay another day. Having gained little from the business part of this trip, I would at least redeem the *pleasure* part.

Mid-morning freeway traffic barreled along at seventy-*plus.* Some *lōlō* maniac in a Buick cut in front of me, nearly forcing my rented Taurus onto the shoulder.

L.A. freeways always shatter my nerves. I scanned the radio for some soul-soothing Hawaiian music–Brothers Cazimero, Mākaha Sons, Iz, Sistah Robi, Keali'i Reichel, Cecil & Kapono, and *da kine*–predictably finding none. I settled instead for a call-in talk show hosted by an eloquent British man. Coincidentally, the topic was raising the California speed limit to seventy-five. *Bad idea.*

Not surprisingly, some callers were all for it. "Cars are better built today," they said. "Freeways are safer," etc. I wasn't buying it. Some callers sounded pretty brash. Others were *huhū*–very upset.

I tried to imagine such a talk show broadcast in the islands. Callers would be more soft-spoken, I imagined, if not more humble. In Hawai'i being loud and opinionated is not necessarily considered a virtue.

More brash voices battled on that L.A. talk show. *Later.* I switched off the radio and mulled over my perplexing case: Adrienne doesn't speak to her sister for five years, then upon her death inherits everything. She blames the accident on Sara's ex-husband, but has hardly a shred of evidence. Parke's visiting Kalaupapa the day before Sara's fall looks suspicious, but how in the world could he have killed her? Only one witness, Milton Yu, admits to knowing J. Gregory Parke. Another witness, Heather Linborg, though she denies it, probably knows him as well. But none of this, so far, leads anywhere. If Yu and Linborg did conspire with Parke, the same problem: *how could they have committed murder with a mule?*

Maybe Adrienne simply had too vivid an imagination. Maybe she felt guilty about her sister's death. It was hard to tell. I was beginning to wonder which was the bigger puzzle: the case or the client? I decided to put the whole thing out of my mind for next few blissful hours that I hoped to spend with my *'ono wahine*, Niki.

Before reaching the LAX airport turnoff, I left the San Diego Freeway at Venice Boulevard and drove west to Pacific Coast Highway. Descending jets hung in the airport's glide paths like glinting beads. I pulled into a Chevron station and topped off the Taurus, then drove through a McDonald's for a Quarter Pounder with cheese and a shake. Just thinking about seeing Niki again had made me hungry. *Yes!* And the two thousand miles of ocean between Adrienne and me had begun to assuage my guilty conscience. Besides, Niki and I had never pledged undying faithfulness. We'd only known each other six months.

I sped along the Coast Highway toward Niki's condo, balancing my burger and shake. My pulse quickened. My heart thumped. I got crazy just thinking about my *fun-fun-fun* California blonde. Less than a mile's drive south brought the back bay of Marina Del Rey, a pleasure boat harbor only two miles from the airport and lined with yachts, trendy restaurants, and swanky condos.

Marina Del Rey is a lively place. In these condos, among sun-tanned boaters, reside pilots and flight attendants from the many airlines that serve LAX. Most are young and single and on the prowl, the married ones having moved to inland suburbs to raise their families. Niki lived in such a condo called *La Casa Nova*. Though flight attendants frequently share their apartments, Niki had told me she lived alone, preferring privacy and quiet to catch up on sleep after long night flights.

La Casa Nova I'd never seen, but she had described it to me in such detail that I easily found the rambling stucco buildings across from the bay-front "Chowder House" restaurant with a dozen slips filled with yachts. I parked my car and approached the condominium on foot. Its wrought iron security gate, as I expected, was locked. Since I wanted to surprise Niki, I didn't use the intercom. I waited for a resident to come along with a gate key.

Within minutes two arm-in-arm lovers, both in airline uniforms, strolled up as if walking on air. The bleach blonde woman and her glazed-eyed pilot were oblivious to me. The gate opened and I followed them in. They never looked back, beating a hot path to their apartment.

The lushly landscaped *La Casa Nova* consisted of a several stuccoed wings built around a pink, heart-shaped swimming pool. *Nice touch.* The effect reminded me of a Japanese "love hotel." From Niki's letters, I recalled that her apartment was "309-F." I wandered the grounds until I found the "F" wing, huffed up outdoor stairs to the third floor, then hurried past the first few doors. My pulse was racing when I reached "309-F." To drive Adrienne Ridgely and her case far from my mind, I chanted a love mantra: *Niki–Niki–Niki.* When Niki's door eventually opened, I was sure my face would reveal nothing but *Pure Stoke* at seeing my *'ono wahine.*

Imagining the totally *out of control* scene that would soon take place in Niki's condo—*Ho!*—I knocked on "309-F" and listened with anticipation to oddly heavy footsteps approaching the door. A smile tightened on my face. *"Niki–Niki–Niki."* I uttered the mantra under my breath. The dead bolt cranked and the door swung open. My smile fell.

Standing before me was not my lovely Niki, but a pink-eyed, stubble-cheeked airline pilot in his mid-forties who looked as if he had just crashed-landed on an overnight flight. His pilot's uniform was wrinkled, his ruddy face was shadowed by those mostly gray whiskers, and his eyes on closer inspection appeared not just pink, but bloodshot.

"Who are you?" I asked, more than a little curious.

"Captain Jacoby," he said in a gravelly, brusque voice. "Who the hell are *you?*"

I glanced inside the dark and disordered apartment. "Where's Niki?"

"Flying to Denver." The bedraggled pilot looked me up and down. "Why do you want to know?"

"Niki is . . . ." I hesitated. "She's an old friend."

"Yeah, I've heard that one before," he smirked.

The more this rumpled pilot talked, the less I liked him. My fists involuntarily clenched. *Like beef?*

"Niki doesn't pick up guys on airplanes anymore," the pilot glowered. "She's mine."

"What makes you think she picked me up?" I shot back.

"Look, you're not the first lovesick puppy to come sniffing after her." His stance spread. His arms hung loose, ready to fight.

"Lovesick puppy!" I puffed up my chest. About to swing on him, suddenly I saw myself being played like a chess pawn. The image looked comical. *What a stupid gremmie I've been!* I began to feel more sorry for this red-eyed pilot than for myself. After all, my worries about Niki were over. His worries, well, had maybe just begun.

"How long have you two been a couple?" I asked in a more conciliatory tone, expecting to hear: *"Only a month . . . ."* Or a few days, more or less.

"A year this November." The pilot's fists remained clinched.

"A *year?*" Suddenly I lost my wind. *So she's been sleeping with the two of us all along? The whole six months I've known her?*

"When did you meet Niki?" Captain Jacoby kept in his fighting stance.

"On Maui," I said wistfully. "Long ago—so long I can't recall."

The pilot relaxed his stance and grinned. I was no longer a threat. "Who should I tell her stopped by?"

"Never mind." I turned and started walking down the stuccoed hall. "She probably wouldn't remember me anyway."

IX: Chapter Thirteen: Surfing at Canoes

When Kai lands in Honolulu after his brief trip to Los Angeles, he returns to his studio apartment and finds a Star-Bulletin *story about a missing fisherman, who turns out to be the victim's assistant, Baron Taniguchi. In earlier drafts, however, Kai goes surfing at Canoes to unwind. This nearly three-page interlude contains Kai's painterly description of a sunset in Waikīkī. Though an amateur painter at best, he tries to convey the glow on the water that he also feels inside himself. The last line containing "MISSING FISHERMAN'S TACKLE FOUND" is the point where the passage would have connected to the published version.*

(cut from)
thirteen

My plane landed in Honolulu at five. I knew only one way to clear my head. I rode a shuttle into Waikīkī, dumped my bag in my apartment, then toted my longboard to the beach. The sun hung low over the teal horizon—slipping slowly toward the surf.

I paddled out by the Moana Surfrider to that fabled wave-riding spot called Canoes. Catamarans, outriggers, and booze cruise boats having already cast off for their sunset sails, the beach lay empty except for a few late swimmers near shore. The ocean and air temperatures were the same—about eighty. *A warm bath.*

As the sun dipped into amber tinted surf, the shimmering sea actually glowed. When I gazed toward Diamond Head, luminous in the flood of golden light, the rolling swells next door at Queens reflected like mirror. Only a few dapples on the liquid glass from a Trade Wind breeze proved I wasn't dreaming.

As this amber calm settled on the lineup, I became one small figure on a vast impressionist canvas of glowing ocean and surf and sky—a sunset scene rendered in warm, passionate hues worthy of Renoir or Monet. *Awesome.* To me, each wave rolling in was an incredible gift. Sets of two and three welled up over the reefs, each comber luring a half dozen surfers. The swell rose slowly, feathering rather than breaking top to bottom. Despite the crowds, I got some nice rides.

When the sun's amber arcs faded into a pearly twilight, it was time to head in. *Pau.* The next set looked promising, but I let the first wave go by. Several surfers paddled for it. The second wave came and lured those missed the first. I let the second one go by too.

Only a pair of us remained for the third wave. I stroked hard and dropped in, feeling my board scoot forward in a rush. Rising to my feet, I noticed I had company. The other guy suddenly dropped in right in front of me. *Hey, you!* I had every right to knock him off his board. Instead I gave him stink eye and turned into a broken section of the wave. When I glanced back he was walking the nose when his board pearled and shot tail-first—*Look out!*—into the air.

The wave was mine. It reformed and I rode it all the way in.

Longboard dripping under my arm I stepped with light feet up Waikīkī Beach—*stoked* from my last ride—toward the grand, white-columned Moana Hotel, home for forty years of radio's "Hawaii Calls." All along the beach, oceanfront bars and restaurants were hopping. The aromas of rum and coconut milk and pineapple filled the air. Slack key guitars twanged. A Hawaiian singer crooned in falsetto that classic kitsch tune still haunting me from my breathless evening with Adrienne: *"Moonlight and you in blue Hawaii . . . ."*

The song's effect was different now. Melancholy, it made me feel. And lonely.

Returning to my flat at the Waikīkī Edgewater, I took Niki's photo in her string bikini at Sunset Beach from the night stand and slid it face down into the drawer. *My California blonde . . . .* I wasn't angry anymore. I just preferred not look at her.

"Good-bye, Niki," I said. "We had fun."

My eyes moistened a little, but not for long . . . . Later, as I mechanically went through my ritual of reading Honolulu's two daily papers, a story caught my eye. MISSING FISHERMAN'S TACKLE FOUND.

X: Chapter Twenty-Four: North Shore Surfing

Before his fateful interview with the prime suspect in Sara Ridgley-Park's murder, Kai says: "With six hours until the interview with Dr. Goto, I did something not every detective would understand. I drove to the North Shore and went surfing." The next line puts Kai in an elevator to the doctor's office. No further mention of the North Shore or surfing. In earlier drafts Kai recounts his surf session in detail and tells us about his Hawaiian cousin Alika, his surfing mentor. Alika plays a more prominent role in Wipeout!, *where his knowledge of big wave riding aids Kai in solving the case. Here Alika appears in an interlude, rather than in the central action.*

(cut from)
twenty-four

With six hours until the interview with Dr. Goto, I did something not every detective would understand. I called cousin Alika, grabbed my longboard, and headed for the North Shore.

Someone might reasonably ask, "Considering all that hung in the balance, how can you paddle out into the blue?"

My answer: "This is how I survive."

At Sunset Beach Alika and I stroked hungrily into the lineup. A shoulder-high swell was forming up nicely into hollow, right-breaking peaks. Not bad for October.

I don't usually trouble Alika with the details of my cases. He is a tall, sinewy, soft-spoken Hawaiian whose focus on surfing is nearly complete. Like his father, my namesake Uncle Kaipo, Alika is a born waterman. He has managed to live his entire thirty-eight years on the North Shore, working as a life guard, coral diver, chef, spear fisherman, and surfing instructor. He and his wife, Malia, and their two *keiki* still reside with the Kealoha *'ohana* who, as I said, first adopted me when my parents died.

Alika knows all the North Shore breaks as well as anyone, but Sunset Beach is his special place. Out here he is my mentor. And on *these* waves, sometimes you need one.

Sunset can be a very intense, complex break with a quickly changing lineup, wicked rip currents, and a dangerous shallow coral reef. You don't want to go out here unless you really know what you're doing. Too often I hear surfers from town or the mainland boast, "I'm going to ride Sunset (or Pipeline or Waimea) just to say I did it."

My response is always the same: Sit on the beach and watch the veterans. Where do they paddle out? Where do they sit in the lineup and take off on the wave? How do they battle the soup and deal with the rip? And when their session is over, where do they paddle in to shore? Until you can answer these questions, you're not ready to get wet.

There is a big difference, you see, between waves in town and in the country. A four foot swell at Sunset is equivalent to about six feet at Waikīkī. The reason for this is that country waves are thicker and carry more water. And are more unpredictable. Due to their larger mass and erratic nature, when country waves break they can peak up suddenly and dramatically. Nearly *doubling* in height. Regardless of the surf forecast, bigger than anticipated sets may abruptly loom on the horizon and break far outside. As the boiling white water rolls in, all you can do is "duck dive" or "turn turtle." After a set or two crashes in front of you, you're totally *gassed*.

Welcome to the North Shore!

The rips and unpredictable swells at Sunset that present problems in winter were fairly under control today. Or so it appeared. This was October when the North Shore can be flat as a lake. But we got lucky. A consistent four feet. And as we soon discovered—*higher.*

"Outside!" Alika pointed on the horizon to an ominous swell—a rogue wave—more than twice the size of any we'd seen. This maverick was deep forest green and peaking fast. *Ho, brah!*

We paddled like scared gremmies. *Arms throbbing. Adrenaline pumping.* The wave's towering face was nearly vertical when we got there. Too late to drop in. *Way too late.* With one last gasp I paddled straight up over the top.

"*Swoosh!*" went the curling lip, blowing back a white gauzy spray that hit me like hard rain. "*Boom!*" The wave exploded. *Lucky I wasn't sucked over the falls,* I consoled myself. Then I looked around. *Where's Alika?* He was gone. Had he eaten it and got washed into the reef? This could be bad. *Very bad.*

Then in the distance near shore I saw the tiny figure of a surfer ripping on the very rogue wave that had almost pummeled me. *Alika.* Impossible!

"You miss one good wave, brah," my cousin said as he paddled back—*stoked*—into the lineup. When I asked him how he caught it, he patted me on the back and simply said: "Show you *bumbye.*" In other words, soon enough.

Between sets later that afternoon we sat on our boards contemplating a thousand tiny sunbeams on the dappled sea. My eyes got so accustomed to these dancing lights that the ocean surrounding them began to look black as midnight. An optical illusion, no doubt. But the apparent blackness of the sea got me thinking. Suddenly I had a strong premonition about the Moloka'i case.

Gazing across the inky water at a coconut palm on shore, I imagined one of its nuts falling and spewing sweet liquor on the sand.

Like that fallen coconut, this case was about to crack wide open.

XI: Chapter Thirty-Two: Wrap Up

After Kai visits Adrienne in hospital on the last page of the book, he heads for Waikīkī and goes surfing—feeling restored, balanced, and free. In earlier drafts, the ending wrapped up two additional strands in the novel: The case of deadbeat dad, Leonard Souza, and Kai's long distance relationship with Niki. Not to mention one last call (and one last joke) from his offbeat attorney friend, Tommy Woo. This wrap up, comprising about two pages in draft, was condensed into one paragraph in the published book. This is another example of sacrificing details of Kai's life and work for the sake of a fast-moving read.

(cut from)
thirty-five

Later that Friday morning I drove to my Maunakea Street office and called Mrs. Souza.

First, she gave me the bad news: Her deadbeat ex-husband was up to his old tricks–threatening her by phone and loitering on her property, despite a restraining order. Though the last person on earth I felt like confronting again was Leonard Souza–especially brandishing his gleaming serrated blade–I told her I would be right over.

Then Mrs. Souza gave me the good news: My presence was not required. She had called the police several times. Finally they arrested her ex for violating the restraining order.

With the scourge of Leonard Souza off my hands, I headed back to the Waikīkī Edgewater with one thing on my mind.

Go surf, brah!

Inside my apartment the red light on my answering machine blinked. Whoever the caller was I didn't want to know. I slipped on my board shorts, peeked under the bandage on my tender shoulder, then headed out the door.

When I stepped into the hall and was about to lock up, curiosity got the better of me. *What the heck?* I walked back inside and pushed the blinking red light. Two messages:

"Hey, Kai," said the wry, sardonic voice, "did you hear the one about the Chinese, Filipino, and Hawaiian astronauts?" *Tommy Woo.*

"You told me that one already, Tommy," I thought aloud.

After a punch line *still* too politically incorrect to repeat, Tommy said: "Seriously, how about spaghetti this Monday— same old place?"

Yes, dinner with Tommy. Long overdue. I would call him back later.

The second message went like this:

"Well, hello there . . . ," said the coy and sexy voice. *"Guess who?"*

It was Niki—my California girl.

"Good news!" She sounded excited. "My request to change flight bases from L.A. to Honolulu was approved . . . ." A pause for effect. *"Isn't that great!"*

Niki's prepared little speech went on. *Fun-fun-fun.* I peered at the STOP button on the answering machine that if pushed would kill the message. Then I wondered: *What happened to her airline pilot?* Had Captain Jacoby flown the coop? Had he returned to a wife and kids in some inland suburb far from Marina Del Rey?

"Anyway . . . ," Niki hesitated, sounding slightly guilty, "we've *really* got to talk. Sorry I've been so slow in returning your calls. It's these damn flights to Indianapolis . . . ."

I punched STOP. Niki's voice cut off.

Within minutes I was paddling out to the fun little breakers at Canoes. My left shoulder throbbed when I stroked and the first splash of salt water stung. Soon the frothing soup from an inside set tore off the bandage. The sun streamed down on the open wound. By the time I had paddled outside to the lineup, my shoulder felt numb. *No fear. No pain.*

Sitting on my longboard waiting for a good set to roll in, my mind roamed. I wondered what I would say to Niki. Actually, I knew *what* I would say to her. How to say it was the question.

Then I thought about the *hui.* Someday I would no doubt hear again from Manny Lee, if not from his moke pals. But not right away. The *hui,* and Manny especially, was in hiding. Everyone had crawled under a bush, trying to avoid the media and the Feds.

And I had gone surfing—not to recollect this bizarre case like Sherlock Holmes puffing on his pipe—but to restore the balance in my life. After all, I am the *surfing* detective. I had been a detective, only, for too long.

It was high time to catch a wave.

XII: Epilogue

In the following epilogue that was deleted from the published book, Kai explains the meaning of the figurines he found on the Kalaupapa trail in chapter five and he recounts his somewhat melancholy last days with Adrienne — and how her image and voice still haunt him. The epilogue may have disappeared because it effectively ends the relationship between the PI and his client, whereas the published version leaves open the possibility of them continuing to see each other.

Epilogue

Two last points require brief explanation to close the case:

First: If you are still wondering about those tiny religious figurines by switchback 16 on the Kalaupapa trail, Sara's lovesick ex-husband, J. Gregory Parke, repeatedly denied putting them there. So did Rush McTower, who surprisingly returned my call. On a hunch I phoned Johnny Kaluna on Moloka'i and asked if he'd seen anyone hiking down the trail to tend the shrine. There was a long silence. Then the *paniolo* confessed. Kaluna himself had placed the figurines, rosary beads, and *maile lei* there. For Sara or his mule, he didn't say. The red roses, he claimed, he knew nothing about. They remain a mystery.

Second: My client remained in the islands nearly a month after her release. Adrienne gave me a bonus for uncovering the *hui* conspiracy behind her sister's accidental death. On that bonus we spent three long weekends together on Maui, Kaua'i, and, her favorite, Moloka'i. Though she thoroughly enjoyed her tropical vacation, as she called it, Adrienne concluded she would always be only a sojourner in the islands. She was a *New Englander* through and through. Boston was her home.

By the time she left in early November I was impossibly hung on her. We kept in touch for a while by phone and email. But as each month passed, we talked less. The five thousand miles and six time zones that separated us eventually took their toll.

I still half expect her to knock on my office door one dewy, fragrant morning—glacier eyes beaming—with some new bizarre case for me to solve. Once I thought I heard her voice calling to me through the door.

But I was only dreaming.

ABOUT THE AUTHOR

Chip Hughes earned a Ph.D. in English at Indiana University and taught American literature, film, writing, and popular fiction at the University of Hawai'i at Mānoa. He left the university in 2008 to write full time. His non-fiction publications include *Beyond The Red Pony: A Reader's Companion to Steinbeck's Complete Short Stories*—also translated into Japanese; *John Steinbeck: A Study of the Short Fiction*; and numerous essays and reviews.

An active member of the Private Eye Writers of America, Chip launched the Surfing Detective mystery series in 2004 with *Murder on Moloka'i*. The second book, *Wipeout!*, followed in 2007. The third, *Kula,* in 2011. Other titles, in various stages of development, include *Murder at Volcano House, Barking Sands,* and *The Maui Masseuse.* The series has been optioned for television. More at http://surfingdetective.com.

Chip lives in Windward O'ahu with his wife and two retrievers. He surfs when time allows.

Made in the USA
Charleston, SC
05 November 2011